CORDELIA CODD

It's Alive!

CLAIRE O'BRIEN

ORCHARD

ORCHARD BOOKS
Carmelite House, 50 Victoria Embankment, London EC4Y 0DZ
First published in 2015 by Orchard Books

ISBN 978 1 40833 573 4

A CIP catalogue record for this book
is available from the British Library.

1 3 5 7 9 8 6 4 2

Printed and bound by CPI Group (UK) Ltd, Croydon, CR0 4YY

The paper and board used in this book are made
from wood from responsible sources.

MIX
Paper from
responsible sources
FSC® C104740

Orchard Books is an imprint of Hachette Children's Group
part of the Watts Publishing Group Limited,
an Hachette UK company.

www.hachette.co.uk

To everyone who has a
BIG DREAM

I'm sitting in Bessie's Bakery with my best friend, Fiona. She's only been my best friend for a few weeks but this is the PERFECT time for her to pop into my life because she saved me from being LEMON-SOLO-ON-MY-OWNIO. My last best friend, Dru, went back to Seattle with her family – a trillion miles away on the other side of the world, in the USA, and I was so LONELY and miserable without her that I thought I might just slip down a drain and die there.

I still email Dru a lot and she'll always be my FABULOUS, FARAWAY FRIEND with a great big place in my heart but everyone needs a RIGHT-HERE-EVERYDAY FRIEND too, don't they? That's why I call Fiona my best friend.

We're eating ENORMOUS slices of chocolate cake and slurping lemonade while we have a MASSIVE moaning session.

'It's OUTRAGEOUS!' I say, and do a tiny lemonade burp behind my hand.

'It's completely unfair,' Fiona agrees, stabbing her cake with a fork.

I'm frowning so much that I can nearly see my own eyebrows. 'We worked REALLY hard. We did EVERYTHING that we were supposed to do.'

Fiona sighs deeply. 'But we've still been rejected.'

This is all about the school Halloween Cabaret, the most fun, exciting and interesting school show of the year. Fiona auditioned to sing a solo. She practised and practised and PRACTISED an old song called 'Monster Mash'. Her singing is very good, but I DID tell her NOT to try adding any dance moves – she's an excellent singer but not an especially good dancer. She didn't listen to me, of course. I love Fiona more than chocolate, so I forgive her completely for ignoring my advice but she couldn't resist adding some turns and wiggles, which made her forget the words of the song and she had to go **hum-dee-hum-hum** through some of the lines. The words didn't come back to her in the right order and it all went muddled and quite EMBARRASSING. I could tell that Mr Gampy, our Drama teacher, wasn't impressed and now he's asked Fiona to be a backing singer for Jason instead of doing a solo, which is SO DISAPPOINTING for her.

Jason is the star of EVERY show at Wellminster Community School. He sings so perfectly that he could be in an opera or probably win EUROVISION. I wanted to make his costume because Jason likes to dress up as a lady when he sings and I'm REALLY good at ideas for glamorous dresses. I'm going to be **the *⋆⋆ GREATEST ⋆⋆⋆ costume designer in the history of cinema** when I'm older.

My dress design was SPECTACULAR. I got my idea from a film called *Bride of Frankenstein*, which was made in 1935. Well…actually, I just saw the DVD case in Mum and Dad's collection. I'm not allowed to watch it yet because it has a fifteen certificate. This is RIDICULOUS and INFURIATING but my mum and dad are super-strict about what I'm allowed to watch. Mum took the DVD away and put it in her 'NOT UNTIL YOU'RE OLDER' box.

Luckily, I found some photos from the film in a library book. The actress, Elsa Lanchester, wore a long white dress that hung all the way down to the floor from ENORMOUS shoulder pads. The sleeves were bandages that wrapped round and round her arms and then dangled down, and she had a TALL, sticking-up hairstyle, like a painting of an Egyptian queen.

I came up with something very similar that I could make from an old bed sheet. It was possibly the BEST costume idea I've EVER had! I probably deserved a *★★ CREATIVE GENIUS AWARD ★★* for it and Mr Gampy loved it but Jason decided that he wanted his mum to make his dress instead of me! How

misery making

is THAT!

Just to make me feel even more DEPRESSED, Mr Gampy has asked me to do zombie costumes for the older kids who are going to be serving drinks and snacks at the cabaret. ZOMBIE WAITERS! Where's the glamour in those? I managed not to cry and just mumbled, 'OK, that's fine,' but as soon as I got out of school and was with Fiona I burst out BLUBBERING and we agreed that we needed cake and lemonade and a chat at Bessie's. We're both allowed to come here

for a little while after school sometimes. I texted
Mum and Dad:

> Wll b bk on 6.15 bus. Emrgncy grls
> mtng wth F @B's. Cxx

Fiona hasn't cried at all. She's very tough about
these things. But she's completely FED UP.

'Shall we go to Mason's before you get your
bus?' she suggests. 'We could do with some giggle
therapy.'

I agree, 'Yes, giggle therapy is DESPERATELY
needed.'

We SLURP the final dribbles of lemonade
and put our pocket money together to pay for
everything then head over to Mason's, the greetings
card shop just opposite the bus station.

First we read ALL the cards with rude jokes
in them and try desperately hard to keep our
giggling quiet because the lady who runs the shop
doesn't like people reading all her cards and not
buying any. It is nearly IMPOSSIBLE not to
giggle out loud – Fiona has to hold her nose and
kneel down on the floor to stop herself laughing
and she looks SO funny doing this that I can't

keep my giggles in either and I have to pretend that I'm having a coughing fit to disguise the sound.

When we've calmed down a bit we have a competition to find the WORST card in the shop. These are the soppy cards with rubbish poetry inside. Fiona finds a HUMDINGER. It has a cartoon drawing of a girl in a long peach-coloured dress that looks like a nightie. She is standing in a field full of daisies with her back turned but is peeking over her shoulder from under a peach-coloured parasol with a frill around it. She has HUGE cartoon eyes and her hair is perfect chestnut curls that reach below her waist. Fiona tries to read it but she can't stop laughing.

'To my darling daughter...'

She pretends to be sick because she HATES soppy stuff, then continues:

'HAPPY BIRTHDAY'

She opens it and reads the poem, trying to sound serious:

> You are as pretty as a rose,
> (giggle giggle)
> I like your tiny, turned-up nose,
> I love your sweet and pretty smile,
> (giggle)
> You are my perfect, darling child.'
> (helpless giggle)

'That is total *pants*,' she says, 'I can do better than that,' and she recites her version:

> You are as hairy as a bear,
> Your eyebrows stick up in the air
> I hate your long, green wriggly nose,
> It looks just like a garden hose.'

And we can't control ourselves any more. We laugh like gurgling drains until the shop lady shouts, 'Out you go, you two. I don't need you in here. Out!'

So we stuff the card back in the wrong bit of the shelf and leave, laughing all the way to the bus stop.

I don't know what I'd do without Fiona. I love her SO MUCH that sometimes I feel like she is almost the same person as me. On the bus I think of something I need to text her about even though we've just said goodbye and we'll see each other again in the morning:

Do u nd a cstme 4 bng a bckng sngr?

★ **Fiona** to me:
Mr G sez we MST wr a blk drss. He wz v strct abt tht.

★ **Me** to Fiona:
I hv 1 tht u cn brrw!

★ **Fiona** to me:
XXTHKS c u 2mrwXX

Our house is an old pub called the Jug and Monkey. It's in the middle of a DEEPLY BORING village called Heckaby, about a trillion miles from anywhere interesting or glamorous. Dad is turning it into a cosy gastro pub that will serve beautiful food. He's an AMAZING cook.

There's an old barn at the back of the pub that Mum is going to make into a little cinema. It will be called Heckaby Picture Palace and we'll show lovely old films there, and funny films for children, too. My parents have a HUGE collection of DVDs.

Mum is getting ready for YET ANOTHER inspection by some official people about something called BUILDING REGULATIONS (how boring does that sound!) She is up to her EARS in paperwork. Trying to get permission to open a cinema is UNBELIEVABLY complicated. There are tons of rules that make it difficult and Mum gets INTERROGATED by lots of people wearing suits. You would think that they suspected her of planning to run a terrorist training camp or build a skyscraper with a secret rocket launcher inside it but ALL she wants to do is show lovely films and sell snacks.

Sometimes Mum wants to drop the WHOLE plan but I'm very strict with her and tell her that she must NEVER GIVE UP because running a cinema is her BIG DREAM, and big dreams always take a lot of hard work. I know this because when you want to be **the** [*]★ **GREATEST** ★[*] **costume designer in the history of cinema** you have to practise your drawing EVERY day. So that's what I do.

While all the building work is going on Mum and I are staying in the MICRO-TINY cottage that is stuck to the side of the Jug and Monkey. Very soon, we'll be moving to the big flat upstairs, over the restaurant. It's nearly ready and I can't wait to get settled in my new bedroom.

As soon as I step inside I hear Dad shouting from the pub kitchen. It's just the other side of our wall so the sound travels into the cottage. I go through the door that joins the cottage to the pub and sit down at the kitchen table where he's been experimenting with recipes. Dad is ALWAYS experimenting.

Neither of my parents seem to notice that I've come home. This is normal, I'm afraid. They're a bit OBSESSED with their plans and I am seriously FORGOTTEN ABOUT sometimes.

Dad is in the middle of trying to get the wobble on his crème caramel just right but he has stopped and is looking at Mum with his face all pink and angry, shouting, '**You must be joking?** *No way! Your mother* **cannot** *stay here now!*'

Oh no! Alarm bells are ringing in my brain.

'Is Granny Twigg coming to stay?' I ask, but no one answers.

Granny Twigg (GT) is Mum's mum. She's the grumpiest gran in the universe.

Mum bites her lip and says, 'Sorry, John, but what could I do? She's on her way.'

Dad swears VERY BADLY and doesn't seem to have noticed that his crème caramel has turned out perfectly, so I ask, 'Can I try that?' and he pushes it across the kitchen worktop to me without saying anything. Sometimes you have to make the most of a yummy food opportunity so I finish the crème caramel while Mum and Dad carry on arguing.

'You're too soft with her!' Dad says, still loudly but not shouting now.

'I know, I know,' Mum agrees, scrunching her shoulders up, 'but she hasn't been in touch for weeks. Maybe she wants to apologise for how she behaved last time we saw her…make friends…you know?'

Dad screws his nose up and says, 'Apologise? Your mother? I doubt it. She just wants to come and criticise everything we've done.'

Then Mum gets a bit tearful because she knows

Dad's right. None of us has EVER heard GT (Granny Twigg) say anything friendly or kind.

GT hasn't spoken to Mum for WEEKS because she went into a MAJOR SULK after her sister, my Great Auntie Deidre, left the Jug and Monkey to Mum when she died, instead of to her. She said some very hurtful and unkind things to Mum. Dad doesn't let GT get away with being horrid. They have some VOLCANIC arguments.

Mum is dabbing her eyes with a hanky, saying, 'I can't put her back on the train and send her home, can I?'

Dad starts banging his pots and pans around, pretending to tidy them up.

I call out, 'The wobble on the crème caramel is perfect!' hoping it will cheer things up, but they don't answer me.

When Mum and Dad argue I get upset, too, because I'm worried that Dad will go away again, like last year, and that Mum won't have him back this time. The upset starts to make the crème caramel turn over in my tummy. It's mixing itself up with the lemonade and chocolate cake from Bessie's and now I feel a bit sick. I really want Mum and Dad to be friends all the time but their relationship is very TURBULENT – the dictionary says that this means 'disorderly or confused, not calm or controlled'. That describes them pretty well.

Mum and Dad are Not Quite Together (NQT) because Mum is still angry with Dad for leaving us last year and disappearing to London. She isn't quite ready to let him share the house with us again, even if he is VERY SORRY. He's been living in a caravan in the back yard all summer and Mum says he has to stay there until all the building work on our house is done.

Adding together the NEGATIVE EVENTS of today, which are:

a) Mum and Dad arguing
b) My grumpy granny arriving any minute
c) The **outrageous** rejection of my dress design for Jason
d) My best friend being **relegated** to backing singer

today is looking worse than a potato squashed by a tractor. It has been a TRACTOR MASH day. Thank GOODNESS I have Fiona to make me smile.

I traipse upstairs to my room, feeling that my family is a DISASTER and that I will probably never get to make REALLY good costumes. I change out of my school uniform into my jeans, which are getting much too short. When I tell Mum that I need some new jeans or my ankles will be freezing this winter she says, 'There's no money for any new clothes except school uniform,' so I have to keep wearing wellies and tucking my jeans in so no one will know that they're too short. I am a fashion CATASTROPHE at the moment.

Mum soon calls me down for a FAMILY CONFERENCE.

'Dad and I have been talking,' she begins.

'It sounded more like arguing,' I tell her.

Mum pulls her **I'm so sorry** face, which looks like she is saying **'eek!'** She and Dad both pull this face when they know they have done something that is BAD PARENTING, like shouting at each other when I'm sitting there.

Dad starts with, 'We've sorted things out about Granny now.'

'OK, what's the plan?' I ask. 'PLEASE tell me she's changed her mind and isn't coming.'

'Now then, Coco,' Mum says, frowning. (Only Mum and Dad call me Coco.)

Mum explains that GT is definitely coming but she **does not need to know** that Mum and Dad aren't sharing a room at the moment. While GT is here we must PRETEND that Dad is just TEMPORARILY sleeping in the caravan to make room for her in the house.

'You'll have to sleep in the big bed with me,' Mum says, 'and we'll have to put Granny in your room.'

'No WAY,' I yell. 'I'm nearly thirteen. I need some privacy.'

'I know it isn't perfect, Coco,' Mum says, 'but we'll all have to shuffle up for a few days.'

'Can't I sleep in my new room in the flat?' I ask.

Mum and Dad both shake their heads.

'It's not ready yet,' says Dad, 'the electricity isn't switched on and there's no hot water up there.'

Mum says that I can move the television and some of the film collection and all my sewing and drawing things into the tiny spare room in the cottage, so that I will have somewhere private to sit and draw and watch films, but I'll still have to sleep in her room because all that stuff will fill the spare room and not leave any space for a bed.

'Couldn't Dad share with you?' I suggest. 'Then we could put Granny in the caravan.' I'm thinking that this might help Mum and Dad to be friendlier with each other AND give us a bit of distance from GT.

Dad thinks this is a good idea but Mum just raises her eyebrows, gives him a strict stare and says, 'I don't think so.'

I am wearing my MARDY PANTS about giving up my bedroom. I mean, HONESTLY! How come GT gets MY bedroom ALL TO HERSELF?

However, Mum and Dad are clearly facing a crisis and need me to cooperate. It's ABSOLUTELY true that GT must NEVER KNOW that Mum and Dad are Not Quite Together (NQT). If she knows this then she'll try and bust them apart completely, and I worked VERY hard to get them nearly together again. I even had to go to London to fetch Dad (a whole other long story) so I'm not going to let my grumpy granny spoil things.

'And let's all agree,' says Dad, 'that there will be

no arguments in front of her. We must show a *united front.*

He's right. GT must believe that Mum and Dad are completely IN LOVE AND BEST FRIENDS and that I'm the PERFECT CHILD.

This plan makes us do some RIDICULOUS things. We only have one hour before Mum has to pick GT up from the station so we work fast. Dad puts most of his clothes into Mum's bedroom to make it look like he normally sleeps there. He hangs two of his jumpers over the chair and piles some recipe books on the bedside table, like they are waiting to be read. His socks soon get mixed up with mine and I have to balance my books about films and costumes, and my sketchbook and drawing pencils on top of his cookery books, which makes a DANGEROUSLY high and WOBBLY stack on the table. My head could be SQUASHED in the night by a BOOK AVALANCHE.

I am just about to tell Dad off about this situation when he calls up the stairs, 'Here she comes!'

'Drat!' I didn't even have time to call Fiona and tell her what's going on.

2

I'm dreading having GT around the house. I can
hear you saying, 'Cordelia! Pull yourself together!
What could be so terrible about a little old lady,
especially your own granny?'

Grannies are cuddly and bring cakes and give
you extra spending money when your mum and
dad aren't looking, and generally spoil you a bit,
right? Not this one! This granny is quite a different
species. She's a GROUCHY MOUNTAIN OF
CARDIGANS and she's stepping out of Mum's car
at this very moment, just when things are already
SUPER STRESSY at home.

But there's something different about her. She
looks smaller than I remember, thinner, and she's
using a walking stick. Mum calls me to come and
help with GT's bags. I go outside and pick up her
HEAVY suitcase, then I give GT's icy cheek a little
peck. She doesn't seem to recognise me. She used
to look at me like she was sniffing, with her nose

screwed up, but this time she just looks a bit blank and muddled.

Dad is standing close by. Mum shakes her head and frowns at him. I hear her whisper, 'Something's wrong. She's very confused.'

GT's blank look changes to a scowl, as if she's trying to remember who Dad is and it's annoying her that she can't work it out. I don't say much apart from, 'Hello,' because GT usually snaps at me when I speak. Mum guides her inside, through the pub, so that she can see all the hard work that has been done to renovate it. GT sniffs the air and looks around at our newly decorated, beautiful, inviting, cosy gastro pub.

'Just as I thought,' she says, but doesn't explain what she means.

I think I hear Dad growl and grind his teeth together. He whispers to Mum, 'She sounds the same as ever to me.'

Mum takes Granny through the side door to our MICRO TINY cottage and takes her upstairs into MY bedroom. I follow them, put down the case I'm carrying and pick up our ginger tom cat, Mr Belly, who has been snoozing on the bed. GT immediately brushes imaginary cat hairs from the duvet cover and tuts loudly. I remind myself that I'm supposed to be a PERFECT CHILD and resist the temptation to tell her not to be such a FUSSY OLD FLAPPER. Instead I give a cheerful smile, stroke Mr Belly and say, 'I hope you'll be comfy in here, Gran.'

She doesn't say any of the usual polite things that you or I would say, like, 'I'm sure it'll be lovely,' or, 'Is this your bedroom? Thank you for letting me use it, I'll be ever so careful with your things.' Instead she just looks me up and down, and says, 'You're taller.' This is the first time that she seems to recognise me. Then she dumps her HIDEOUS handbag on MY bed.

I DO NOT like being reminded that I am a lanky giraffe girl. I long to be petite and curvy, like Alice and Juliette at school but before I have time to get annoyed Mum calls upstairs, 'There's a pot of tea ready,' and we all gather in the kitchen.

GT sits on the chair that Dad usually has. Mum and I don't say anything about this because it would be rude and when Dad comes in he just clenches his teeth. I can tell that he's doing this because his jaw and cheekbones go tight. He finds another chair and pretends he is perfectly comfortable on it, probably so that he doesn't look like a fussy pants in front of GT.

'Still drinking awful weak tea, I notice,' says GT, as Mum pours.

Mum stops and puts the teapot down.

'I like mine weak,' I say, to let GT know that I intend to stick up for Mum. 'You can pour mine, Mum.'

'Weak for me, too,' says Dad.

GT narrows her eyes at him. Mum fills our cups and then gets out some ginger biscuits, puts them on a plate and passes them around.

'Haven't you any with chocolate on?' asks GT as she takes TWO ginger biscuits.

'Sorry, no,' says Mum. 'I didn't have time to get to the shop today.'

'No, I don't expect you did,' says GT, crunching on her ginger biscuit and looking up at the cracks in our ceiling. 'Fixing this place up will take every minute you've got. At least I don't have that to worry about.'

'Yes, it's hard work but we're enjoying it,' says Mum. 'Shall I pour your tea now?'

GT gives a sharp little nod.

Mum is very good at not getting FLUSTERED

by GT's mean little comments but I think the hurt gets stored up inside her and that's why she has a big cry every now and then. Dad and I are more likely to have MASSIVE EXPLOSIONS of temper. I'm learning not to do this but having GT around is going to be what Mum would call a CHALLENGE. If I don't explode with temper I will deserve a gold medal for CONTROLLING MY OWN BRAIN.

'How was the train journey?' Mum asks, dunking her ginger biscuit in her weak tea (the way she likes it).

GT stares into her teacup for a moment, quite a long moment. When she eventually looks up she's frowning.

'What train journey?' she asks.

Her face has changed from looking bitter and mean to lost and muddled again.

Mum frowns. Dad frowns. I frown. We are ALL confused.

'The train journey here,' says Mum, gently.

Gran looks around the room. 'I didn't come on the train,' she insists. 'Your dad brought me. He'll be back tomorrow.'

My grandpa died before I was born so I HOPE

he doesn't turn up tomorrow, driving his old car. That would be WELL AND TRULY SPOOKY.

'No, Mum,' *my* mum says softly. 'You came on the train, don't you remember?'

GT looks cross and snaps, 'Don't argue with me, I know how I got here.'

Mum looks at Dad. Dad looks at Mum. He shrugs his shoulders and makes a surprised expression with his eyes like he's saying: 'What is *wrong* with her?'

GT stares into her tea again.

'What's she going on about, Mum?' I whisper.

Mum pats my hand, saying, quietly, 'Gran's a bit tired and confused, that's all, Coco. Don't worry.'

GT doesn't hear this. But I'm worried. She isn't just mean and grumpy, she seems to be going DOTTY in the head, too.

I'm really glad when I can get away from all the TEA and TENSION downstairs and hide in the tiny spare room that is now crammed full of my 'art essentials'. We couldn't fit the computer in here so it's just outside on the landing. First, I send a text message to Fiona.

> GT arrvd! Shs gn wyrd. Tll u mr tmrw.
> Cx

Later, I'll go back downstairs and see if I can get some more information from Mum and Dad about what ON EARTH is going on with GT but right now I need some peace and quiet and I MUST contact Dru (her full name is Drusilla Drummond-Steinway) and tell her about the day's GRIM events. She is always wise and OPTIMISTIC and gives great advice.

It's still the middle of the day where Dru is because her time is eight hours behind ours, so she probably won't be able to reply for a while.

One of the MANY unfair things in this house is that I'm still not allowed to use ANY networking sites. Fiona is online ALL THE TIME but Mum says, 'I want you to write in proper sentences and learn to wait for a reply, like people used to do with real letters.'

'USED TO DO,' I say to her. 'USED TO DO. Past tense, Mum. EVERYONE is on some kind of network now.'

'I'm not,' is all she says. 'And your dad's not.'

I explained that this is because they are both quite old and a bit strange but she wouldn't budge.

Whenever I mention my need for an ONLINE PRESENCE, which is QUITE often, she rolls her eyes and says, 'Not until you're thirteen. That's what we said and we're sticking to it.'

My thirteenth birthday isn't until almost the end of term. This is like waiting FOREVER, so my communications are stuck in the last century while everyone else is allowed to be part of what's happening RIGHT NOW. Mum and Dad just don't get it. Until a year eight kid is properly online it's like we don't EXIST.

Anyway, tonight I have to get in touch with Dru and boring old email is our only option.

★ **Cordelia** to Dru

Hi, far away friend!

Today has been a **BIG FAT** disaster in two **MAJOR** areas.

I tell her about our costume rejection and about GT arriving and taking over MY bedroom. My fingers **rattle tattle** over the keyboard as I hammer out my moans. Poor Dru, sometimes all she hears from me are complaints. I keep promising to send her good news but I don't ever seem to have much. I finish with:

SORRY SORRY SORRY I'm such a bag of whinges. I WILL send good news **ONE DAY**.
   Love you!
   C xx

I'm so exhausted by bedtime, after all that room shuffling, and the traumas of the Halloween Cabaret AND the strain of trying to be patient with GT, that I'm fast asleep long before Mum comes in and snuggles down next to me, but I have a horrible dream.

In this dream GT has taken over my bedroom COMPLETELY and filled it with her cardigans, which smell of mothballs and strong tea. She has pulled down my vintage film star posters of Audrey Hepburn and Rita Hayworth, and all my colourful cushions and my lovely, sparkly light shade have gone. The warm cosiness has been blown away because she keeps the window open ALL DAY and lets the damp autumn air in. It curls the pages of my sketchbooks up at the corners and blows my pencils around. I try to catch them but they roll away from me and get lost under the bed. I panic and I have to lie down on my tummy to reach into the under-bed dust to get them back, but I pull out a set of dentures and some ENORMOUS old lady knickers instead and THAT'S when I wake up with my PANICKY heart beating like a drum. It is 23.52 according to Mum's bedside clock. Mum is fast asleep. Gradually, my heart slows down and I nod off again.

But at exactly 03.22 I am woken up again, this time by a voice calling in a whisper, 'Deirdre, Deirdre!' I open my eyes and S C R E A M, 'AAAAGH! MUM!'

Mum sits bolt upright with her hair all over the place shouting, 'What! What's happening! What? Coco!' Then she sees what I can see standing at the end of the bed and gasps, clutching her heart, until she realises who it is and lets out a big sigh, saying, 'Oh, Mum! Thank goodness it's only you.'

'Only you!' I say, my eyes still popping out on stalks. 'She nearly gave me a heart attack! I've never had such a FRIZZY FRIGHT!'

GT is standing at the end of the bed with Mum's

big torch shining up from under her chin. It makes her look PROPER SCARY.

Mum pats my shoulder, saying, 'It's OK, she's just muddled again.'

GREAT. Granny isn't just dotty, she's dotty and is wandering around in the night making Halloween faces with a torch. This is DEEPLY UNSETTLING. I may never sleep properly in this house again.

GT hasn't moved. She calls out in a panicky voice, 'Into the shelter, Deirdre! Air raid!'

'Oh dear,' says Mum, 'she thinks it's the war. She's looking for Auntie Deirdre.'

'It's OK, Mum,' *my* mum says to GT, jumping out of bed.

Mum steers GT gently back across the landing. GT keeps asking, 'Where's Deirdre? Where's Deirdre?' and Mum tells her again and again, in a calming voice, 'She's safe, she's safe.'

I help to guide her and I can feel how skinny her shoulders have become. She shuffles back to bed muttering, 'Safe now, we're all safe now,' and curls up on the mattress like a toddler. Mum puts the duvet over her again and in five seconds she is sleeping silently, as if nothing had happened.

'Was she sleepwalking?' I ask.

Mum nods. 'I think so.'

Back on the chilly landing she gives me a hug.

'Sorry, Coco,' she says, 'Granny's not very well. I had no idea she was so muddled. I'm going to call the doctor tomorrow.'

3

Breakfast time is the first chance I get to tell Mum about having to do zombie costumes instead of Jason's dress. Dad has come in from the caravan to use our bathroom. I know this because the old water pipes make a

BUBBLING, CLONKING

sound when anyone takes a shower. This morning it's SO LOUD that we have to speak up to have a conversation.

'Never mind,' Mum says, when I explain the ENORMOUSLY UNFAIR situation about the Halloween Cabaret. 'It's good to try making all kinds of costumes, not just glamorous ones.'

She has a point. Real designers have to build a

PORTFOLIO. This is a collection of pictures of all the different kinds of costumes you can make.

'Whatever you do, just give it 110%,' Mum says, 'and decide you're going to enjoy it.' She rubs my back to cheer me up. 'Before you know it, you might be enjoying it for real.'

'Does that work for things that you REALLY hate doing?' I ask. 'Like Geography homework?'

'It works *especially* well for things you hate doing,' she says, passing me a slice of toast. 'The bigger the challenge, the more you'll learn.'

'So, when you have to fill out all those forms for the council,' I say, spreading butter and then marmalade onto my toast, 'is that what you do? Do you say to yourself, "Right, I'm REALLY going to enjoy filling out this huge, long, pointless and complicated questionnaire?"'

Mum laughs.

'I try,' she says. 'I didn't say it was easy, but what's the point in being miserable about something that you've got to do anyway?'

'So, I should pretend that I WANT to make zombie costumes?' I ask.

'Why not?' she says, pouring us both some tea. 'You might be surprised at the ideas you come up with.'

I'll have to give this idea some time to sink into my brain, but I don't get the chance right now because GT has come down for breakfast.

'I hope you've made the tea properly this morning,' is all she says.

Poor Mum, I don't think she's going to have an easy day AT ALL.

My friend Joe is on the school bus, as usual. Sometimes we chatter like magpies and other times, like this morning, we just sit next to each other and stare out of the window without feeling like we need to talk. It's lovely to know a boy who is just a friend. After Fiona, Joe is probably the person I like most at Wellminster.

I used to DREAD getting on the school bus because of Ruby MacPherson, the QUEEN OF THE BULLIES, and Becky Freemantle, who was always lurking behind her, backing her up. Joe stuck up for me when they picked on me HORRIBLY. That was only a few weeks ago. Ruby even HIT me once. She threatened to put me in hospital and she wrecked a skirt that I was making. Ruby and Becky were a POISONOUS PAIR. Luckily for me,

Ruby moved house, so she doesn't get this bus any more, and she had a HUGE argument with Becky recently so they can't STAND each other now.

Joe is a bit older than me so he isn't in my registration group. We say goodbye when we get into school and I go to meet Fiona in our usual spot on the low wall by the teachers' car park – she lives in Wellminster so she only has a five-minute walk to school.

I immediately tell her all about GT and her strange behaviour and the OUTRAGEOUS business of having to give up my room for her. She agrees that it's a TERRIBLE INJUSTICE that I've had to give up my room and that we ALL need some privacy at our age, and she invites me to come for lots of sleepovers while GT is staying. Thank GOODNESS for Fiona.

When we get to registration Alice Fong and Juliette Peters are already there. They're a bit like Fiona and me because they walk around giggling together a lot of the time. Aled Coombes is shy and skinny and is good friends with Jamie McAllister, who suffers from really bad spots and is already taller than most of the teachers. Samantha Tuttington is always alone and looks more Gothic and depressed every week. Jamila Stevens is bouncy and enthusiastic and Becky Freemantle is still NOT speaking to Ruby McPherson, who sits at the back in every lesson, texting and picking at her nail polish.

The best thing about year eight so far, apart from having a BRILLIANT best friend, is that our new registration tutor is the **BEL♥VED** Miss Wallcott. We were supposed to have a new teacher called Mr Finnegan but he hasn't arrived yet. Someone said he's been kidnapped by pirates and someone else said he's lost in the jungle in South America, and that he is always having dangerous adventures, like Indiana Jones in *Raiders of the Lost Ark*. I've even heard that he has a limp and a scar on his cheek from fighting off bandits. Whatever the truth is, Mr Finnegan is certainly a *Mystery Man*.

Meanwhile, we're happy with Miss Wallcott. She's also our History teacher and everyone is BESOTTED with her. Besotted is a good word I found recently. It means that we all ADORE her. She is like a sunny day.

My two favourite subjects at the moment are History and French. I like History because of Miss Wallcott but also because it's full of stories, and stories need costumes, so I can spend a lot of time wondering what everyone was wearing during the English Civil War and the Industrial Revolution.

French is important for me because lots of French words are used to describe clothes and fabrics. Last year I visited the Victoria and Albert Museum in London with Dad, and I started making a list of these words and their pronunciation in a special notebook. Some of my favourite French words for types of fabric are:

Voile (vwal)
Crepe de chine (crep de sheen)
Le toile (le twaal)

and:

Le velours (le vel-oar).

And some of my favourite words for clothes are:

La chemise (la shem-eese) – a shirt
La lingerie (la lan-shay-ree) – underwear
La jupe (la joop) – a skirt

and:

Le gilet (le jee-lay) – a waistcoat

I'm also collecting other French words to do with sewing, like:

Trop juste (tro joost) – too tight
Les ciseaux (lay see-so) – the scissors
L'aiguille (l'agg-weey) – the needle
Coudre (coo-dr) – to sew
Couper (coo-pay) – to cut

And then a few other random words that I'm trying to use in conversation to make me sound more sophisticated like:

Démodé (day-mod-ay) – old-fashioned
Trés chic (tray sheek) – very smart
Jamais (sham-ay) – never
Toujours (too-jor) – always

Avant-garde (av-on-gar) – making new art, being the first to try something

And:

Voila! (vwah-la) – there you are!

Our French teacher is Mrs Crowther-Dupont who has a Yorkshire accent and knits HIDEOUS jumpers during the class. She mostly gives us worksheets to do and then ignores us, which is ABSOLUTELY NOT the sort of teaching we should have. But French is so important for my BIG DREAM, and I like the sound of it so much that I'm not going to give up and stop trying. Instead, I'm going to work SO HARD that I'll get a BRILLIANT mark and then I might get moved into the top group with Mrs Moreau. She's a proper French person and doesn't look like she would be interested in knitting. She is *toujours trés chic*.

But today is Tuesday, which starts with Science. We're doing a lot of Chemistry this term, which Fiona is EXCEPTIONALLY good at so I let her take the lead when we do experiments. I'm always a bit nervous that something might catch fire if

I'm in control but she is SUPER CALM about that sort of thing. She wants to be a pyrotechnic engineer when she's older. I didn't know what that was until she told me – it's someone who designs firework displays. What a FANTASTIC job!

Fiona is particularly happy today because we are learning about combustible materials. This means things that burn and explode, which is quite important for her to know if she's going to be a pyrotechnic engineer.

Science has NO costumes, which makes it difficult for me to get interested, but Mrs Jesmond, our Science teacher, does use different fabrics to demonstrate what burns easily, so that is a TINY bit interesting, I suppose. Some of them make a TERRIBLE STINK when she sets fire to them with a Bunsen burner. Bits of melted fabric fly out of the window and stick to the ceiling. I'm sure this is against some sort of health-and-safety rule.

At the end of the lesson Fiona volunteers BOTH of us to stay behind and help Mrs Jesmond to scrape some combusted materials off the floor tiles.

As we scrape I tell her Mum's advice about the Halloween Cabaret and she agrees that it's probably best to accept the things that Mr Gampy has asked us to do and to make sure we do them FANTASTICALLY well, if we can.

So, Fiona decides to be the BEST backing singer she possibly can be and I decide that if I've got to make utterly unglamorous zombie costumes then I'll make sure that they are the MOST disgusting examples of the walking dead they can possibly be without actually putting people off their crisps and lemonade.

After morning break we have some time in the Head Space. This is the BEST room in our ENTIRE school. All the shelves and chairs and tables were once the insides of an old-fashioned library. That library was closed down but a kind lady in Wellminster bought all the furniture and paid for it to be put into a temporary building in a corner of the school grounds. This was a stroke of GENIUS.

There are no computers in the Head Space and you have to leave all your electronic gadgets outside in a locker. Inside, everything is made of wood and there are comfy seats, big tables that you can spread maps and books out on and LOTS of quiet corners for reading.

Most of us enjoy the chance to escape from

computers for a while and relax with a book. Books don't have advertisements that POP UP. They don't make PING PING noises when they want to distract you with something, or have CLICKETY CLACK keyboards. Books don't crash or keep asking if you want to SHARE things with the world. People who say that kids don't like books and peace and quiet are WRONG ALMIGHTY – they know NOTHING about our brains.

In the middle of the Head Space there's an old wood-burning stove with a chimney that goes out through the roof. It will soon be cold enough to light it and Mr Gurniman, our English teacher, says we can sit round and warm out toes on the fireguard as long as we are sensible and don't 'burn the place to the ground'.

The only rule in here is that we have to work on our own, quietly. However, I'm always curious to know what other kids are reading because this can reveal interesting and surprising things about their personalities. REVEAL is a word I've been using recently. It means 'to show or uncover' but it sounds more mysterious.

I can't see what EVERYONE is reading because there are thirty-three of us in my class, but I can get a good peek at some people's choices. For example,

Bossy Becky Fremantle has pulled out a star chart from a big drawer where the posters and maps are laid flat. She is spreading it across a table and is in her own little stargazing world.

Aled has an ENORMOUS book about earthquakes and volcanoes opened on another table and Jamie is sitting on a rug by one of the windows looking at a map of a bike race called the Tour de France, because he's MAD KEEN on cycling.

Miserable Samantha heads for the vampire stories and Alice is near the sports section. Ruby sulks in the corner, picking her fingernails and refusing to choose a book but Juliette is reading *Everest, the Killer Mountain* – a strange choice for a girl who is scared to climb a rope in the gym.

I always go to the shelves where I know the best costume books are and Fiona likes to find stuff about Chemistry and Physics. Today, I'm looking for zombie pictures to try and get some ideas

flowing

through my brain. I find a big, heavy book that might have what I want and settle down in a leather armchair with a lamp above it, which I switch on. Just behind me, Peter Skanski is browsing in a section called 'Great Composers', which doesn't surprise me AT ALL.

Peter has just joined year eight. He was away at a special boarding school for super-brainy kids last year but has just moved to Heckaby with his mum. I don't know why. His life is another one of the mysteries of Wellminster Community School.

Peter is SO clever that it's annoying, especially when he gets arrogant about it. ARROGANT is another word I'm using recently. It means someone who thinks they are clever and important. Arrogant boys are NOT attractive to sophisticated girls like Fiona and myself. We call him PETER POMPOUS PANTS behind his back.

I'm quite peacefully turning the pages of *Hollywood Horror* when Peter interrupts, which he isn't supposed to do – this is a SILENT time.

'That looks interesting,' he says in a whisper, so that Mr Gurniman won't hear.

'Yes,' I whisper back, 'but I'm looking for zombie pictures and there aren't many in here. It's mostly vampires.'

'Have you tried looking in the index?' he asks. HOW PATRONISING!

PATRONISING is an excellent word. It's

when someone sounds like they are being kind or helpful but actually they are acting superior, like they think you are an imbecile. This is VERY annoying. My face is flushing scarlet, I can tell, because I feel hot.

'Of course I have,' I whisper back, harshly, like I'm spitting gravel at him.

I turn to the front of the book.

'No,' he says, smiling in an infuriating way, 'that's the *contents*. The index is at the back.'

I know this but he has flustered me and now I'm going redder and redder. Why doesn't he just GO AWAY!

Instead, he makes things even worse by asking, 'Do you know the difference between the contents and the index?' like he's my teacher!

'Yes,' I hiss. 'Of course I do.'

'Tell me what the difference is, then,' he asks, with his most arrogant smile.

'Contents go at the front and the index goes at the back.' I say. 'Now, stop bothering me, will you?'

Peter rolls his eyes and instead of going away he sits down next to me so that he can whisper even more quietly. 'Yes, yes, But what are their separate *functions*? What do they *do*? Do you know *that*?'

How DARE he start giving me a quiz about books? How DARE he try and humiliate me!

'Of course I know,' I say, and pretend to go back to *Hollywood Horror* even though I am now COMPLETELY distracted.

And I DO know the answer but he has annoyed me SO MUCH that I need a moment to bring the answers to the front of my brain. In the meantime, I am thinking that I would like to smack his cheeky face – this would be a VERY bad idea. I would just get into terrible trouble and, besides that, I have promised myself that I will control my temper.

I take a deep breath and calm down, then look straight at him and whisper, 'Are you asking me because YOU don't know the answer or because you think that I don't know and you're hoping to make me feel like an idiot?'

Peter sits back in his chair. He looks surprised that I'm cross. How can he NOT see how annoying he is?

'I'm trying to help,' he whispers.

'Well, you're going about it in completely the wrong way,' I tell him.

He looks more than surprised now. He looks ASTONISHED and BEWILDERED at this news.

'Am I?'

'Definitely, totally and ABSOLUTELY the wrong way,' I add, also in a whisper, but very firmly, to make sure he understands. Then I give him one of my mini-lectures, which is hard to do in a quiet voice but I manage it.

'You've just plonked yourself down next to me, disturbed my reading and started testing me. I hope you don't have ANY ambitions to become a teacher because ALL children will hate you INSTANTLY.'

He looks down at the floor and says, 'I really was just trying to help.'

'Well, you didn't.'

By this time the answer has made its way to the front of my brain so I add, 'And the contents is usually a list of chapters but the index is an alphabetical list of names or subjects with page numbers. May I get on with my reading now?'

'Yes, sorry, yes,' he says and shuffles away. He has a big balloon head but I have just popped it with a pin. GOOD.

I carry on reading but about ten minutes later he comes back with a book I haven't seen before.

'Sorry,' he whispers. 'I know I'm an annoying twit sometimes.'

I glance up from my book, 'Yes, you are.'

He is blushing a tiny bit when he says, 'I found a zombie picture you might like.'

He hands me the book.

'Thank you,' I say, but only VERY quietly and I keep my expression serious even though I can feel myself ALMOST forgiving him for being obnoxious and I want to smile – but I don't – when I see what a GREAT picture he's found.

'May I sit here?' he asks, pointing to the chair next to me.

'OK,' I agree, still looking serious, 'as long as you keep quiet.'

4

The first rehearsal for the Halloween Cabaret is at lunchtime today. I tell Fiona about Peter as we hurry along to the Drama Studio. She agrees that he is probably the MOST annoying boy in the school, then she has to dash to the loo before the rehearsal starts.

I find a place to stand in the busy hall and watch the other kids arriving. After a few minutes I look over to where the singers are starting to gather on the stage. Fiona has joined them. She waves to me. I wave back, but then I have to sit down before I fall over with SHOCK.

There are three backing singers – that bit is normal. Fiona is looking excited and pretty, but standing next to her are THE OTHER TWO. I can't believe it! My eyes squint and then go all popping out. This is just AWFUL. The other two backing singers are Ruby MacPherson and Becky Freemantle, my ABSOLUTE enemies.

Well, as soon as Fiona realises that she has to
sing with THEM, she'll walk away, that's certain.
She won't sing with two girls who made my life
MISERABLE a few weeks ago, will she?

I wait for Fiona to tell Mr Gampy that she can't
possibly continue. I expect she'll come and sit
next to me, to show how she sticks by her BEST
FRIEND. It will happen any minute now. I'm
just waiting…I'm still waiting…I'm still waiting
when they start to sing some lines together. I don't
understand. She is just getting on with it, as if they
are two PERFECTLY OK girls. Isn't she thinking
about how I must feel? Doesn't she remember that
just a few weeks ago Ruby SLAPPED me across
the face and threatened to put me in hospital? How
could she do that? I am SO upset that I storm out of
the Drama studio.

Fiona sits down next to me in afternoon
registration as if NOTHING had happened. How
can she not know that I'm upset? She eventually
notices that I'm not looking at her and asks,
'What's wrong, Cordelia?'

I wish I could stay calm but I just can't. I am an EMOTIONAL JELLY and I sound really snappy.

'How could you POSSIBLY sing with those two, Fiona?'

Fiona frowns and looks like she has no idea what I'm talking about.

'It doesn't matter, does it?' she says. 'I'm not going to hang out with them or anything.'

I manage to squeak out, 'Of course you are! You'll be rehearsing with them every day this week.'

Fiona's cheeks flush scarlet, a sure sign that she's getting impatient with me.

'That doesn't mean I'll be their friend,' she says.

But I don't believe her. I waited so long for a best friend and I don't want to lose her. I start to panic and say things I don't mean.

'How could you BETRAY me like this? You're being selfish.'

'It's not selfish,' she says, getting quite stroppy. 'It's **you** who's being selfish, selfish and clingy. I want to sing in the cabaret and that matters more to me than who I have to work with. Don't be a drama queen about it, Cordelia. It's just a few songs.'

'I'm NOT being a drama queen!'

'Yes, you are. You **really, really** are, Cordelia.'

Then I say a really STUPID thing.

'You CAN'T sing with them if you're my friend.'

Fiona pauses, takes a breath and says calmly,
'Well, maybe I won't be your friend for a while then,'
and goes to sit next to Becky.

My heart crumbles into little pieces.

I feel numb and half asleep for the rest of the day.
I can't concentrate and my tummy is churning
around. I'm lost without Fiona. She doesn't even
look at me for the rest of the day AND she stays
sitting next to BECKY FREEMANTLE.

I concentrate REALLY hard on the French
lesson in the afternoon, to try and take my mind
off what has happened. I'm sure Fiona will come
and apologise soon. I'm SURE she'll realise that
I'm right and will come back to me. She should say
sorry, shouldn't she? Because I am right, aren't I?

But she doesn't speak to me at afternoon break,
or in the last lesson, which is Geography with Mrs
O'Donnell. The lesson is something to do with
oxbow lakes, which are made when rivers meander

on their way to the sea. I am not really listening and I miss the part where they stop being rivers and become lakes. Oh dear! I feel sick and lonely and angry all at the same time. How COULD Fiona just abandon me like this? Should I say sorry first? But what would I be saying sorry for? I don't understand. She's the one who's hurt me. She should say sorry first, shouldn't she?

On the school bus Joe is already sitting with someone so I sit alone and close my eyes, hoping that I might open them and find that today was just a bad dream, like GT's dentures and pants being under my bed. How much worse could the day get? Well, I soon find out.

I decide to watch some old zombie films from Mum and Dad's collection to take my mind off ANOTHER awful day. Perhaps if I can get some ideas for costumes I won't feel so miserable about arguing with Fiona.

Most of our films are in boxes on our landing at the moment so it takes me a while to find the ones I want. I watch about twenty minutes of *King of the Zombies* and ten minutes of *Plague of the Zombies* and stop the DVD when I want to sketch something. Neither of these films is scary AT ALL. In fact, they are a bit *pants* but I have to watch them for research.

Normally, watching films gives me brilliant ideas but tonight I'm stuck. Even films and costumes aren't interesting at the moment. NOTHING is interesting while Fiona isn't my friend.

I keep checking my phone, waiting for her to text me a big SORRY. I wish she would realise how much she's upset me and hurry up and apologise because my sadness is as HEAVY as cold cauliflower cheese. I almost text her first but then I stop myself. I still don't see why I should. I'm sure she's in the wrong. Best friends are supposed to stick together ALWAYS, aren't they? And she shouldn't have sung with Becky and Ruby, should she?

Dad eventually calls me down for dinner. I don't feel hungry but then I smell today's impressive experiment. The scents of garlic and sausage, tomatoes and herbs waft up the stairs and my appetite comes back.

For a while GT seems perfectly normal (grumpy) again. She complains that Dad's cooking is 'too rich', and says, 'We old folks can't eat fancy food, our stomachs need something simple.'

She just CAN'T control her complaining brain and she isn't even TRYING to be polite. She could at least have said, 'Thank you,' and left the bits she can't eat. And no one told her that she had to clear her plate, but she did, she scoffed the LOT and then had TWO helpings of Dad's apple crumble for pudding, so it will be her own fault if her tummy hurts later.

After dinner, Mum goes out to the barn with her torch to check on the building work and I'm allowed on the computer to see if Dru has sent me a response. She has, and there's a photo attached of her with her friend, Esther. They are both suntanned and smiling. Dru's hair used to be frizzy and sticky-out but it's calmed down a bit now and settled into bouncy waves. She's wearing shorts in the photo and I'm sure her legs are getting longer. I notice that her knees don't stick out in a knobbly way, like mine do. I'm a bit jealous, partly because of her knees but mostly because she and Esther both look so FLIPPING HAPPY.

★ **Dru** to Cordelia

    Hi Cordelia! WOW! It sounds like

your granny will be needing help from now on. Do you think she knows there's something wrong with her and that's why she came to stay, so that she can be near your mum?

News from here. My lovely Aunt Zillah is really sick. She has to go into hospital for a heart operation. We think she'll be OK but she's worried about missing all the Halloween pumpkin. Mom says, 'No more pumpkin pie for you, Zillah, or any kind of pie. That's why you're sick – too many pies.'

About the costume thing – you will make the most **FANTASTIC** zombies! Don't worry about Jason's dress. There will be other dresses.

Love you!

Dx

I write back telling her that I'm REALLY sorry about her Aunt Zillah and I hope she gets well quickly because I know Dru loves her LOADS. Then I let her know that I'm LETTING GO of doing the costume for Jason, so she needn't worry.

But the stuff that is really bubbling up inside, the stuff that I HAVE to write down to stop it EXPLODING inside me, is my argument with Fiona and how I'm waiting and waiting for an apology but, meanwhile, I'm SO lonely. So, once again, I end up writing loads of my miserable moans and sending them to Dru.

I use the web cam on the computer to take a selfie to send to her but those pictures always make me look like I'm staring into the back of a spoon – my face goes bulgy and egg-shaped and I look like an alien, so I delete it.

Later, I sit up in bed trying ONCE MORE to have ideas for zombie costumes, but nothing will SQUEEZE out of my head. Eventually I fall asleep with Mum reading a soppy, romantic book next to me. I wish she'd be soppy and romantic with Dad instead of just reading about make-believe husbands.

The next thing I know I jump SO HIGH with

another FRIZZY FRIGHT that I nearly hit the ceiling. Drawing pencils cascade ALL OVER the floor making a terrible RATTLING sound as they hit the bare boards. I must've nodded off while I was working. I'm still wearing my dressing gown. Just like last night, the clock says 03.22. GT is standing at the end of the bed again, staring with her scary torch-lit face. I shake Mum to wake her up and GT shouts, 'Air raid! Quick, Deirdre! Into the shelter!'

GOOD GRIEF! Is this going to happen EVERY NIGHT?

Mum and I take Gran back to bed, staying as calm and gentle as we can and reassuring her that Hitler ISN'T coming and that Deirdre is fine. She's soon curled up fast asleep again.

'We have to remember,' says Mum, yawning and cuddling my shoulder as we shuffle back across the landing, 'that when Gran thinks it's still the Second World War she is only about three years old in her mind. That's the age she was during the Blitz.'

'She's having sort of "time slips" in her brain, isn't she?' I say.

Mum nods and pulls the covers over both of us.

I sometimes have time slips when I'm CONVINCED that I should have been a costume designer in Hollywood in the 1950s. I don't suppose that's QUITE the same thing, though.

♥

I am downstairs in the morning before GT is awake so Mum and I have a nice, quiet breakfast. I wonder if I should tell her about Fiona? No, I won't, because I'm sure we'll be friends again by lunchtime. Fiona will come and talk to me, or text me, or something. Mum doesn't need to be bothered about it. She's got enough on her plate with GT.

'You won't let Gran bully you, will you, Mum?' I ask. 'Even is she is a bit muddled.'

Mum gives me a little smile and sips her coffee. 'I promise to stand up for myself,' she says.

The toast POPS up behind her and she leans across to pull it out of the toaster, then starts buttering it.

'She isn't as strong as she used to be,' Mum continues, 'as well as being confused, her bones hurt a lot and her eyesight isn't so good any more. We'll have to make allowances for her, I'm afraid.'

'You're already EVER SO patient with her and you're EMPATHETIC.'

'That's a good word,' says Mum.

EMPATHETIC is another of my new words. Our big dictionary says that it means 'to understand and share the feelings of another'. I'm trying to do this, but sometimes people just infuriate me and I can't work out why they are being so ANNOYING. It will be almost IMPOSSIBLE to empathise with GT while her behaviour is so bizarre.

'I can't imagine being old,' I tell Mum.

She looks up from her plate and smiles.

'And that's exactly how it should be,' she says. 'You're only just getting started in life. You've got a lot to do before you're my age, never mind being as old as Granny.' She points at the clock. 'So you'd better finish your toast and get off to school.'

We were having such a peaceful start to the day that I had forgotten the time, and have to run for the bus still carrying my toast and marmalade wrapped in a piece of kitchen towel.

Joe is already on board, sitting halfway back, smiling and looking healthy from being out on his allotment. Joe loves growing vegetables. When the village flooded a few weeks ago, he was at the allotment and all his plants and his greenhouse got washed away. It was a good thing that he was there because little Mina who lives at Akbar's newsagents had wandered away from her house. She fell in the river but Joe jumped in and saved her. He's a local hero and Mina is the LUCKIEST toddler in the world! It was in the newspapers. Everyone loves Joe now, except Mrs Driscoll from Driscoll's Discount Shop. She doesn't seem to love anyone. She particularly hates schoolchildren. In the summer holiday she accused Joe of stealing from her, which was a MASSIVE fib, so we don't go in there any more.

As soon as I see Joe, I remember something. He likes to recycle things and Dad has told him that he can help himself to stuff from our builder's skip to rebuild his green house. He's coming over tonight to have dinner and pick up some wood. That means he'll meet GT. How EMBARRASSING is that going to be! He's obviously looking forward to it because the first thing he says to me is, 'Am I still invited over tonight?'

I nod. 'It'll be fun,' I tell him, not meaning it at all. 'Except for my gran.'

'Why is that a problem?'

I sigh.

'Well, just don't be surprised if there's a bit of an

ATMOSPHERE at dinner time,' I warn him. 'She's grumpy and strange.'

Joe bursts out laughing. Typical.

'Don't worry, I'll charm your granny with my *charisma*,' he jokes.

I roll my eyes and shake my head. He has NO IDEA what he'll be dealing with.

Should I tell him about Fiona? No, I decide not to because I'm still sure that she'll apologise by lunchtime and everything will be OK. But, of course, it doesn't work out like that.

Fiona sits with Becky in registration and still seems to be ignoring me. What is the matter with that girl? Why doesn't she just come and say sorry so that we can go back to normal? She doesn't look at me at all, not even a glance. Then Becky turns around and gives me a HARD stare when Fiona isn't looking. Now I understand. Becky is STEALING Fiona. She's NICKING my best friend. I bet Fiona wants to come over and make friends with me but Becky won't let her. Or perhaps that's just what I IMAGINE is happening but actually Fiona doesn't

WANT to come back to me. I'm guessing because I don't really know WHAT'S going on in Fiona's head. I just know that I want my best friend back.

Should I talk to Fiona first, instead of waiting for her to come and say sorry? That doesn't feel fair. And I can't talk to her in class, anyway, because Becky will hear and she'll say something HORRID to me, then I'll probably burst into tears in front of her and she'll call me a baby. I'm sure Fiona will come over as soon as she can get away from Becky. Perhaps she's just waiting for a chance to catch me alone and say sorry without being overheard. Yes, I'm pretty sure that's what she's thinking. But, then, perhaps I'm just guessing again, and now I'm not sure at all and I'm feeling impatient as well as upset, so I have to try and concentrate on the next lesson, which is Art, to stop myself from panicking about what I should do.

Mrs Allen, our Art teacher, is round and chubby. She has spiky blonde hair and wears big earrings. She's quite a softie but most of the time her lessons are such fun that no one messes about. Even the kids who think Art is a waste of time behave quite well because Mrs Allen has clever and interesting ways of keeping us all busy.

On each table there are two piles of fabric, one

pile is black and shiny and the other is a luminous, YUK-green colour. There are also sticks of chalk, long rulers and several pairs of big scissors. Everyone starts fiddling with things until Mrs Allen claps her big hands together and calls, 'Hold on! You don't know what you're doing yet.'

Most people pay attention then and put the things down. Miserable Samantha is trimming the ends of her long hair with the scissors.

'Shall I cut it short for you?' says Aled, snipping the air near her hair.

Samantha gasps. Mrs Allen doesn't see this because she is just beginning her demonstration.

'Today we're going to make some Halloween bunting for the cabaret,' she announces.

There are a few groans but I bet most of the class don't even know what bunting is so I don't know why they're already complaining.

'Bunting doesn't have to be neat little triangles,' Mrs Allen explains. 'Our bunting will be more *freestyle*. We just need to tear all this fabric into strips.

'Each strip should be fifteen centimetres wide,' she says, 'and forty centimetres long.'

She draws a big rectangle on the board.

'Use the rulers on the table to measure and mark with chalk before you start cutting or tearing.'

Then she makes a little snip in a big piece of the black, shiny fabric and pulls hard. A FANTASTIC ripping sound makes everyone jump and pay attention. Tearing things up is always fun.

'Make several snips first, fifteen centimetres apart,' she tells us.

Then she demonstrates, SNIP SNIP SNIP.

'Then cut or tear.'

RIIIP! RIIIP! RIIIP!

'Pile the strips up, then measure and mark forty centimetres, then another forty centimetres until you reach the end.'

She scoops her strips up with a FLUMP FLUMP GATHER GATHER noise. Wow! She works fast!

'Then cut them to the right length.'

SNIP SNIP SNIP

'There! Easy! All we have to do now is tie each rectangle onto a string and we have our raggedy Halloween bunting. Michael and Joshua, come and hold up this string for me.'

We all get the idea. The strips are frayed and crumpled – they are PERFECT for Halloween.

'Have a try. Off you go!' says Mrs Allen. 'The table with the most bunting up in one hour gets to leave ten minutes early for lunch.'

When we came into the class, Michael and Joshua's brains were going into sleepy 'standby' mode because they both have minds that don't work properly unless they are using a computer – art and craft activities just seem to confuse them. However, Mrs Allen helps them both to be CREATIVE HUMAN BEINGS by giving them the job of measuring out lengths of string for the bunting to hang from. This means that they have to:

a) stay away from a computer for a while

b) move their hands and body around and do something three dimensional

c) use maths, which they are both quite good at

d) talk to other people, which they are Not good at, so working as a team is excellent practice for them

Mrs Allen is a GENIUS at tricking people into enjoying Art but unfortunately Michael and Joshua get in everyone's way with their measuring because they unwind long lengths of string across the art room. Miserable Samantha gets tangled up when she has to go out to the loo and Alice can't get past them to the cupboard to get more chalk when Aled accidentally steps on hers. Eventually, Mrs Allen sends Michael and Joshua to work in the corridor, which saves the rest of us from getting tied up like parcels.

We are working in groups. Fiona is in Becky's group with Gill and Ahmed and she doesn't look my way at all. I carry on cutting up and tearing the fabric into strips, trying to pretend I don't care. We're all snipping and ripping and chalking and measuring as fast as we can because we each want to be the table that wins. I bring my own lunch, but if you stay for school dinners, being ten minutes early puts you at the front of the queue – then you get the hot, crispy chips instead of the left over soggy ones. Peter Skanski is on my table, working at SNAIL SPEED.

'Can't you go a little bit faster?' I ask. 'Don't you want to win?'

71

'I can't be bribed by ten minutes extra lunch break,' he says. 'My price is higher than that.'

He is obviously trying to sound sophisticated and mysterious but is just annoying the rest of the group.

Aled gets quite narky with him. 'For such a clever clogs, Peter, you can be quite dumb. Do you want the best chips or not?'

Jamila rips her fourth strip saying, 'It's about helping each other, Peter.'

Peter shrugs. 'But I bring sandwiches,' he says. 'Why should I bother?'

Aled looks FURIOUS. For a moment I think he's going to punch Peter, but he manages to hold himself back and just gives Peter a hard-man stare.

'This isn't just about *you*, Peter.' He says, 'It's about working as a team, helping your mates. One day you might need help with something.'

Then Peter Pompous Pants says a HORRIBLE thing. 'I don't think there's anything **you** could possibly help **me** with, Aled.'

What a NASTY SNOB he can be.

Aled is clenching his teeth. He looks Peter straight in the eye and RIIIPS a piece of fabric to show how angry he is, saying, 'You better hope there isn't, Peter Perfect, cos I wouldn't help you now if you were dying of thirst in a desert and I had a spare bottle of water.'

Peter looks down at the table and doesn't say anything else. I hope he's looking down like that because he's DEEPLY ASHAMED of himself. No one speaks to him for the rest of the day. We just COULDN'T, not until he apologises. Not until he learns to be less selfish.

After a while we change groups. When we're all moving around I catch Fiona glancing my way, just for a second. She looks away again as soon as our eyes meet, but she DEFINITELY looked. I'm SURE that means that she's missing me and wants to be sitting with me again. She MUST be thinking that, mustn't she? After all, we're best friends.

I THINK Fiona is about to stop and say something to me but Becky pulls her by the elbow and takes her off in another direction. Why doesn't Fiona tell her to GET LOST? Perhaps I should ask to go to the loo and send her a text while I'm out of the classroom. No, what if Becky saw what I'd written? She'd tease me about it and probably make Fiona send a HORRID message back. Or maybe I just IMAGINED that Fiona wanted to talk to me. Maybe that's just what I HOPED was going to happen. This is all so BLEAK and DEPRESSING.

Peter is in another group now. He's with Michael and Joshua. They have finished measuring string and are wrapping sloppy papier-mâché around balloons. I hope I get to have a go at that, too, because it looks wonderfully messy and you don't get to do that sort of stuff in secondary school very much. The balloon shapes will be made into bright orange pumpkins and hung up with the green-and-black bunting. I think it's all going to look pretty good.

I'm with a group making cobwebs from black wool. Fiona is right on the other side of the art room with Alice and Jamila, so I can't see whether she looks my way.

Luckily, the cobweb making is tricky and involves a lot of knot tying, so we have to concentrate. We're making cobwebs inside old picture frames that Mrs Allen bought from junk shops and sprayed silver.

'I needed a *dexterous* group to do this job,' Mrs Allen says, when she comes over to check our work. 'You're all doing very well.'

'What's dexterous?' Jamie asks.

Mrs Allen jumps up and stops the whole class by shaking a tambourine.

RATTLY RATTLY TINKLY JING!

'Listen up, everyone. New word alert,' she calls. 'Jamie, please fetch the big dictionary.'

Everyone listens when Mrs Allen does a NEW WORD ALERT because, like doing papier-mâché, it reminds us of being at primary school again and we ALL wish we were back there sometimes.

Mrs Allen keeps a big dictionary in the Art room because she says, 'Interesting new words can pop up at any time and we need to be ready for them. They don't just belong in English lessons.'

She writes DEXTEROUS on the white board and asks, 'Who thinks they know the meaning of this word?'

Peter Pompous Pants doesn't put his hand up, even though we ALL KNOW that he will have the answer. He's probably still too ASHAMED to speak.

Alice Fong shoots her hand up and shouts, 'Is it something to do with sugar, Miss?'

Mrs Allen writes DEXTROSE underneath DEXTEROUS.

'Not quite but it sounds similar, Alice. Dextrose is a type of sugar but dexterous is different. Good try.'

Jamie is struggling to hold the ENORMOUS dictionary up. It must weigh as much as three or four laptops.

'Someone who is dexterous has dexterity,' Mrs Allen explains. She writes DEXTERITY next to DEXTEROUS. 'Read dexterity please, Jamie.'

He reads,

'Skill in performing tasks, especially with the hands.'

'Thank you, Jamie. So, a dexterous person is good with their hands. Remember that new word. I think it was worth interrupting you for. Back to work now.'

And she claps her hands together, like big loaves of bread.

We have to use all our DEXTERITY to make the cobwebs and they take ages, but they look great when we add the purple spiders that another group are making from felt and pipe-cleaners. It's lovely doing this sort of art, where everyone works on one big thing. Normally we have to do 'individual projects' that are marked and graded and all the fun is squeezed out. Everyone should get to mess around practising their DEXTERITY with wool and fabric and papier-mâché and paints sometimes. It was fun. It would just have been so much MORE fun if I'd been giggling over it with Fiona.

At the end of the morning Mrs Allen lets us ALL have ten minutes extra for lunch, saying, 'Your work this morning will benefit the *whole* school so I think it's fair that you get to be first in the lunch queue for one day. Off you go!'

We have left behind some impressive-looking bunting, six giant spiders on cobwebby picture frames, some fat, round pumpkins that still need to be painted and Peter Pompous Pants, on his own with his sandwiches.

5

There's no sign of Fiona at lunchtime. I sit on
the wall near the car park again and wait, but she
doesn't come and join me. Normally, I would really
enjoy my sandwiches. Today, Dad has made me a
ciabatta roll with goat's cheese, rocket and pesto.
Not many kids get fancy sandwiches like that, but it
might as well be plain bread and margarine because
I'm just TOO SAD to enjoy it.

After lunch we are in the Head Space again.
Every time I catch Fiona's eye she looks away.
This is getting SILLY. I had to have my lunch all
by myself and she STILL hasn't come to talk to
me. Surely she could escape from Becky for a few
minutes if she wanted to. But maybe she's thinking
the same about me. Maybe she's thinking that
I don't want to make friends. Or, perhaps, even
though she KNOWS that she was wrong and
should apologise, she is enjoying being with Becky
more than with me and has decided not to come

back and be my friend but to stay over on the dark side of the universe. Oh dear! Now I'm REALLY starting to panic. Fiona could become one of the mean girls. How can I save her?

The last lesson is Science. Fiona works with Jamila and I have to work with miserable Samantha who hardly ever speaks. Mrs Jesmond tells her to tie her hair back and she sulks because no one has a hairband to lend her so she has to use a lace out of her Dr. Martens. Then, just to make the day end with a complete COW PLOP, when it comes to tidying-up time Becky stays behind with Fiona INSTEAD OF ME. Did Fiona ask her to? Well, if she did then that's PROOF that she doesn't want to be friends, isn't it?

Now I feel angry with Fiona. She OBVIOUSLY doesn't understand how BETRAYED I feel. I decide to tell Joe, after all.

Joe and I manage to get a seat together on the bus, which is MIRACULOUS because it's packed. It stinks of sweaty trainers and fruit-flavoured boiled sweets – Michael Dunster had a bagful but they've been snatched by big kids and are being passed around. It's also INCREDIBLY noisy in here so we have to raise our voices just to hear each other.

Joe is chatty and enthusiastic about the new greenhouse he's building and the potatoes he's planting but before we have passed the shopping centre on the edge of Wellminster he stops and says, 'OK, I can tell there's something bothering you. What's going on?'

And I blurt it all out. I tell him about my argument with Fiona. I tell him that I'm waiting for an apology because she called me clingy and selfish and a drama queen. And I tell him how she has betrayed me by singing with Ruby and Becky and how hurt I feel, and how depressed I am because I don't know what to do to make her understand what she's done and get her back.

'Just go back a step,' he says, when I run out of breath and have to pause.

'I'm not sure that she needs to say sorry to you, Cordelia.'

That is NOT what I wanted to hear.

'Why not? I'm SO upset.'

'Yes, but maybe you didn't need to be upset,' he says. 'Maybe Fiona choosing to sing with girls you don't like is OK but you can't accept it.'

'How can it POSSIBLY be OK to sing with Ruby and Becky after the way they treated me?' I ask him, feeling red and cross all over again.

'Because it's you that had trouble with them, not Fiona,' he explains.

Joe is watching my face closely. I don't like what he's saying. Why can't Fiona just listen to me? I've told her how nasty they can be.

'So, are you saying that she's right?' I ask, sounding sulky. 'Do YOU think I was being selfish and clingy and a DRAMA QUEEN?'

He shakes his head.

'No, but it sounds like you panicked a bit when you saw that she was singing with them. That probably made you act in a clingy way, trying to control who she sings with. Maybe you should just apologise to her first.'

'But what FOR?' I say in quite a shouty voice.

'For getting wound up when all she wanted to do was sing. Maybe she thinks you weren't supporting her. You know how she loves to sing. Perhaps you need to let her have a bit of space.'

'But she'll abandon me for Becky if they start hanging out together,' I tell him, and I can hear my voice getting squeaky. I'm panicking, just like Joe said. Perhaps I do get in a flap when I think I'm being abandoned, and perhaps getting in a flap DID make me try to hold on too much to Fiona and act a bit control-freaky. Does that mean I'm the one who's wrong? Really?

'So, if I'm the one who's wrong,' I ask him, feeling a bit trembly and fighting back tears, 'how come it's ME that's all hurt and miserable?'

Joe sighs. 'It's not that one of you is right and the other is wrong, exactly, I don't think arguments work like that. Maybe you both got a bit emotional.'

'Maybe,' I mumble.

'I think Fiona is one of the nicest girls in school, Cordelia, it'd break *my* heart if you two chucked away your friendship. That would be a sad waste. One of you just has to be brave enough to talk, even to apologise.'

I stop talking then and sit, staring out of the window, managing not to cry, watching the hedges and houses whizz past and wondering if I'm brave enough to make the first move and try to be friends again, to even say sorry to her. I'm not sure that I am. I need a SECOND OPINION. I need a reply from Dru.

As the bus splashes through the little ford at the

edge of our village I suddenly remember that Joe is going to meet GT and another wave of stress runs through my insides. What sort of weirdness will he see at my house? Will there be shouting and tears? If I'm REALLY lucky GT might have had a big strop and taken herself home. But no such luck.

The first thing I ask Mum when we get through the door is, 'Is she still here?'

Mum glances up from her paperwork and raises her eyebrows, showing that she disapproves of my question.

'If you mean Granny, yes, she's upstairs, resting,' she tells me. Then she turns to Joe, says, 'Hello,' with a big smile and asks him all about his greenhouse and his baby brothers and everyone else in his family, and completely ignores me. A few minutes later Dad comes in and gives me a quick kiss on the top of my head then also ignores me and asks Joe the same questions ALL OVER AGAIN. I wish Mum and Dad made enough time to be that interested in ME.

Joe and I rummage through the skip in our back

yard and find some recycling treasures to go with the wood that Dad has put aside for him. He looks delighted when he finds two old guttering pipes and a window frame. He even gets excited about some worn-out carpet.

'Are you sure you want that?' I ask him. 'It must be soaked with ancient beer. It came out of the pub.'

Joe laughs. 'Old carpet is brilliant for covering your compost heap. It keeps the heat in so everything rots down quicker.'

Joe can find a use for ANYTHING.

Mum is cooking dinner tonight, which is OK, but not quite as good as when Dad does it. GT seems to be having a very long nap so we don't see her until we have washed our hands and are sitting around the table in our tiny kitchen. Mum says it's best to let her rest, so we start dinner without her.

Just as we get chewing, she comes in. We all freeze – there's spaghetti dangling from our forks, halfway to our mouths. GT comes in DANCING! She NEVER dances! Actually, it's more like shuffling, and she's singing an old-fashioned song that goes, 'I'm flying down to Rio de…Janeiro,' with a dreamy smile on her face and her eyes half closed.

Now I've seen EVERYTHING.

Mum blushes scarlet. I don't know if she's embarrassed or just freaked out like the rest of us. None of us has EVER seen GT even looking cheerful, so dancing and singing are WAY off the scale of normal behaviour for her.

Spaghetti slips back onto Mum's plate with a cold SLOPPY-PLIP-PLOP sound. I am hypnotised by GT's little dance.

It's Joe who speaks first, whispering to me ever so quietly. 'I thought you said your gran was grumpy. She looks quite good fun to me.'

Mum is the next one to snap out of her trance.

'Ermm…Joe, can I introduce you to my mother? This is Mrs Twigg.'

'Pleased to meet you, Mrs Twigg,' says Joe, standing up and coming around the table to shake Gran's hand.

GT takes his hand saying, 'Don't mind if I do,' and starts dancing with him, shuffling round the kitchen because there isn't enough space for normal moving around, never mind dancing with an old lady wearing six cardigans – did I mention that she's wearing AT LEAST six cardigans? She looks like a jumble sale – a small DANCING jumble sale with…wait for it…coral pink lipstick! GT wearing LIPSTICK! She used to say that only bad women wore lipstick so either she has replaced her brain with someone else's, or there's been an earthquake in her head and everything has got rattled around.

Joe lets her steer him round the tiny kitchen. I look at Mum.

'Is she a bit tiddly-drunk?' I ask.

Mum shakes her head saying, 'No, she's just very confused again.'

Dad is looking at Mum with his, 'I know I should do something but I don't know what' expression. He is clearly BAFFLED and BEWILDERED.

Mum continues, 'She was asking if I had anything she could wear for the party tonight.'

'What party?' I ask, thinking I might be missing out.

'Exactly!' Mum says as we all wince when Joe and GT shuffle dangerously close to the pan of spaghetti sauce on the cooker. 'There is no party! She hasn't been to a party since 1979.'

Mum takes a deep breath, stands up and holds GT gently by the shoulders, then steers her away from Joe, who is looking a bit dizzy and seems glad to sit down again.

He catches his breath, saying, 'She asked me if I was going to dance with Deirdre when she arrives.'

'What did you say?' I ask him.

Joe looks at his cold dinner, 'I said I'd be happy to if she thought Deirdre would enjoy it.'

I explain that Auntie Deirdre died quite a while ago so it would be a bit strange if she did turn up.

Joe just says, 'Oh, I see,' then smiles and eats his cold spaghetti.

Poor Joe! He must be desperate to get away from me and my BIZARRE family and from his cold dinner.

Mum guides GT to a chair saying, 'All that dancing will be making you hungry, Mum. How about something to eat?'

'Oh all right,' says GT, 'but will there be more dancing later, and champagne! There's usually champagne when Deirdre arrives.'

Mum must be thinking very quickly because she says, 'We've drunk all the champagne, Mum. Time to eat something.'

GT's shoulders droop, 'Oh dear, Deirdre will be disappointed,' she says. But then she gives a big smile and I realise that I've never seen her teeth before – well, actually, she hasn't got any, or rather, she's forgotten her dentures. She calls out cheerfully and raises a bony finger, 'Deirdre will bring some with her, I expect.'

Then she settles into a deep silence and eats a big bowl of half-cold spaghetti. It's like she just switches off and goes into a different world – Planet Spaghetti.

Mum saves us by saying quietly to Dad and me, 'You two take Joe home as soon as you've finished and I'll tidy up. I'll get Mum to bed. We're seeing the doctor in the morning.'

Something REALLY BIG is going on with GT.

'Sorry, Joe,' Mum says, patting Joe's arm. 'This has taken us all by surprise. I hope you'll come again soon.'

'Don't worry, Mrs Codd,' Joe says. 'My grandpa was a bit like this before he…sorry…I mean…'

Joe blushes.

Mum squeezes his arm again. 'It's OK, Joe, I understand,' she says. 'Thank you.'

Was he going to say 'before he died?' Oh dear! I think he was. We move towards the door quietly so that we don't disturb GT, who seems to be unaware of anything in the room now, apart from her plate of spaghetti.

Joe turns to Mum from the door. 'My grandpa…
he was ever so happy. It was like all his worries had
vanished.'

Mum nods again and I think I see her eyes filling
up with tears. She gives a sad little smile. 'Thank
you, Joe,' she says again. 'That's good to know.'

6

Dad, Joe and I lift Joe's recycling treasures into
Dad's van and drive them down to Joe's allotment
where we stack them under a big plastic sheet to
keep them dry. Joe's allotment is a magic garden,
secret and calm. The river races by just beyond the
blackberry bushes at the bottom. When it flooded
and his plants and greenhouse got washed away, his
cosy little shed survived, so he still has a place to go
for quiet thoughts and to read his gardening books.
Joe and I have had some good conversations in
his shed, sharing a flask of tea and some chocolate
biscuits. I sometimes wish I was a bit more like him,
happy to stay quiet and watch vegetables grow.

We drive Joe home as soon as all the junk-
treasure is safely stored. He lives in quite a big, posh
house at the far end of the village with his stepmum,
his dad and twin baby brothers, Sam and Ben.

Dad and Joe look at Joe's plans for his new
greenhouse. They spread Joe's drawings out on the

kitchen table and Dad starts making a list of bits and pieces that Joe still needs to finish it, so that he can put wood and hinges and other useful stuff aside before our builders throw it away. I go and wash my hands in their downstairs cloakroom and as I'm coming out I hear a violin playing. This isn't unusual for Joe's house because his dad is a violin teacher. Instead of going out to work he stays at home to look after the twins – a pair of sticky, messy little nuisances – and teaches violin in the evenings.

Joe's stepmum, Jenny, works in a big bank somewhere and is always rushing around wearing a suit, speaking loudly into a mobile phone. She must be upstairs putting the babies to bed because she doesn't come and say hello, and the STICKY TWINS are nowhere to be seen.

I'm always curious to know who is having a violin lesson. I'm PARTICULARLY curious this time because whoever is playing is REALLY good. There are hardly any SCRAPEY, SCRATCHY noises and it sounds like a proper tune.

I peek through the slightly open door to the room Joe's dad uses for teaching. When I see who's playing I roll my eyes to the ceiling, sigh heavily and give a big tut. I MIGHT HAVE

KNOWN. It's Peter Pompous Pants! He's concentrating hard, so he doesn't notice me and Joe's dad is conducting him gently with his back to the door, so he doesn't see me either.

I stop being a NOSY FALOSY and go back to the kitchen but Dad and Joe are deep in conversation so I sit and wait in the big living room, and flick through a copy of *Vogue* that Joe's stepmum has left on the coffee table. It's mostly adverts but there are some interesting pictures of EXPENSIVE clothes as well. These are called *haute couture* in French – that's pronounced 'oat cootuhr' or something like that. I'm just relaxing, looking at a feature called 'Autumn in Paris' when I am MAJORLY disturbed by Peter Pompous Pants, who has finished his violin lesson.

He mumbles, 'Hello,' then pauses, like he's not sure what to do, before sitting down on the sofa opposite me – you can tell this is a big house because they can fit TWO massive sofas into the living room and still have lots of space.

I mumble, 'Hello,' back to Peter and then try to ignore him but it's difficult. I look up from 'Autumn in Paris'. He's watching me, like he's trying to think of something to say. I can't help it but the first thing that comes out of my mouth sounds quite sarcastic.

'I heard you playing. Is there ANYTHING you're not good at?' Then I realise that I've accidentally paid him a compliment, which I certainly didn't mean to do. DRAT.

Peter gazes up at the ceiling, says very slowly, 'Ermmm, let me think,' then looks back at me and says, 'Not really. I find most things fairly easy once I've got the hang of them.'

He is SUCH a bighead and he brings out the WORST in me. That's why I look him up and down and say, 'Except choosing your clothes. You haven't got the hang of that, have you?'

Peter looks down at his too-short trousers and grandpa trainers and seems a bit surprised. I know I shouldn't be criticising ANYONE'S clothes when mine are such a disaster but I can't stop myself.

Peter looks hurt and now I feel like the meanest girl in the UNIVERSE.

'Are they really awful?' he asks, screwing his nose up. 'I don't bother about clothes much.'

'Clearly!' I reply, thinking, STOP IT! *Cordelia Codd, you are being* HORRIBLE.

I manage to soften my voice a bit and close the copy of *Vogue*, sighing.

'You could certainly do with some fairly urgent help,' I say, hoping this sounds better.

'Perhaps you could give me some advice,' he suggests. 'Would you come shopping with me?'

Well, THAT'S a bit of a shock. Peter Pompous Pants is asking ME for advice! And, of course, I would LOVE an opportunity to restyle someone's wardrobe. It would be brilliant fun. But I MUSTN'T.

'I shouldn't even speak to you,' I tell him.

'Why?' he asks.

My eyes have gone wide and poppy with shock. Doesn't he KNOW WHY? 'Because of what you said to Aled,' I remind him. 'In today's Art class.'

Peter shrugs and pulls a book out of his pocket. He sits back and pretends to be concentrating on it. It's called *The Catcher in the Rye*, by J.D. Salinger and I'm very curious about it but I'm not going to let his interesting book make me change the subject.

'I hope you're going to apologise to him,' I say.

Peter lowers his book and tuts, then says, 'For what?'

Now he's just being a sulky baby.

'For being a horrible snob and for not being

a team player,' I tell him. 'You were completely selfish about the bunting and the chips and most of the class wanting to get to the lunch queue early.

'OK, I was a bit harsh,' he admits. 'But so what?'

'So,' I tell him, quite firmly, 'if you want me to help you sort out your TERRIBLE clothes, you'd better apologise to Aled AND Jamila by the end of school tomorrow.'

And I disappear behind my magazine. I have NO idea whether this will work. Peter might not give a TINY FROG'S FART whether I help him with his wardrobe or not. It's not like I'm his girlfriend or anything. But this is the only thing I can think of to say. Now I'll just have to wait and see.

When we get back from Joe's house it's obvious that Mum has been 'fully occupied' trying to keep an eye on GT. I can't quite believe what I see.

'She's been like this since you left,' Mum tells us.

GT is walking around our newly decorated hallway poking the walls with a dining fork and muttering to herself over and over, 'These walls are damp, we'll have to change the paper.'

Mum looks tired.

'I just had to let her do what she wanted to do,'

she explains. 'If I tried to interfere she got very upset and shouted at me.'

Dad runs his hands over the wallpaper and pulls a HORRIFIED face. His mouth drops open a bit and a little 'uurgh' sound comes out.

'That wallpaper cost a small fortune,' he says.

'I know,' says Mum, getting more hot and bothered. 'I'm sorry. But I just thought that as long as she wasn't hurting herself or anyone else, it was best to leave her alone.'

The wall looks like a perforated tea bag. Dad just shakes his head. It isn't a great time to get cross with Mum. She is clearly NOT having a good evening.

I manage to get online before bed to read Dru's latest reply.

★ **Dru** to Cordelia

Oh no! You fell out with Fiona?? You have **GOT** to make it up. Esther and I argued a few weeks ago. We sat down and had **DIALOGUE**. This is **REALLY** hard because you have to listen and not interrupt while the other person says what they were upset about and how they feel.

It turned out that I was being a bit clingy and getting upset when she went out with other friends. Do you think you might be doing this to Fiona, just a tiny bit???

Will send more news later. Mom is calling me to help her with laundry (boring!)

D xx

There's that word again. CLINGY. But I don't mind Fiona having other friends. Or do I? NO! It's just these PARTICULAR girls I don't want her to hang out with. I mean…I wouldn't get upset if she went around with Jamila or Alice or Penny or ANYONE else…would I? Oh dear! Perhaps I would. Perhaps I really am Little Miss Clingy.

★ **Cordelia** to Dru
Hi! Are you there?
Cxx

★ **Dru** to Cordelia
Yes, the laundry thing was hours

ago. I'm off school 'cos I had to go
to the orthodontist and have my braces
tightened. Ouch!

Dxx

★ **Cordelia** to Dru
Sorry about the braces! I'm sending waves of
sympathy!

I like the idea of having a dialogue with Fiona,
but she won't even look at me. Becky sticks to her
like a BOGIE at break times and I daren't go near
her in case I make a complete TWIT of myself in
front of them.

★ **Dru** to Cordelia
You have to **KEEP TRYING** to talk
with her. I will always, always be
here for you, Cordelia but you need a
best friend who's close by, too. Your
heart must be in little pieces.

★ **Cordelia** to Dru
It is!! A **TRILLION** tiny pieces.

★ **Dru** to Cordelia

Is there **ANY** good news over your side of the ocean?

★ **Cordelia** to Dru

Well...not really...but there's gossip...

And I tell her all about the Peter Pompous Pants Project and how it ISN'T HAPPENING unless he apologises. Dru likes gossip. If I can't send her good news then a bit of gossip is the next best thing.

I finish with:

It's **SO** late now that I'd better get to bed (**YAWN!**) I promise to keep trying for dialogue with Fiona.

Love you!!

C

xx

Very soon, I'm sitting up in bed next to Mum again. She's fast asleep. The bed is still covered with my coloured pencils and sketches. It's pretty cold in here so I have my dressing gown on and my thick, fluffy bed socks.

Chatting with Dru has made me feel that there is a little bit of hope that everything will be all right eventually. Fiona and I WILL be best friends again, but it's going to be tricky to get her to myself for long enough to have a dialogue. And I've got to be very brave – I will just HAVE to be the one to talk first. I'll even apologise. We can't be friends again if we don't talk, can we? Friendship is too important to let my big fat PRIDE get in the way.

Dru must have helped me to unblock my brain because my zombie costume idea begins to take shape. First, I write my ideas down in a list, then I put them on a sort of map with arrows pointing to other ideas and coming off each other like roads. I draw shapes and write names and let my imagination gallop around like a wild pony. I scribble ideas across three big sheets of paper and it would all look like GOBBLEDIGOOK to someone else but it's just my way of letting my creative ideas GROW and FLOW.

GT doesn't wake us ALL NIGHT. HOORAY! I sleep right through to breakfast time and wake up STARVING.

7

GT is her normal grumpy self this morning. While I get ready for school she has a breakfast-time shout at Mum.

'I don't need a doctor! I've got my own doctor at home,' she says, snapping like a crocodile in a cardigan.

Mum is trying to make her understand how weird her behaviour is but GT can't remember dancing around the kitchen with Joe or poking the wallpaper with a fork.

I make my own breakfast and sandwiches then slip away quickly to catch the school bus, where I find Joe and apologise AGAIN for my family.

'Granny can't remember dancing with you last night,' I tell him. 'She's Granny Grouchy again this morning.'

He looks concerned, saying, 'She must be scared. I'd be scared if I thought I was ill and might soon need someone to get me to the bathroom and feed me. When people are scared it can make them angry. Remember what Ruby was like?'

I will NEVER forget. After Ruby was SUCH a bully to me in the summer it turned out that she was terrified of her dad, because he was a MONSTER who used to hit her. She took all her troubles out on kids at school and was violent and scary. So I know exactly what Joe means about people getting angry when they're scared and he's probably BING BANG on the truth button with GT. She's snappy and grumpy because she's scared of getting old, just like Ruby was horrid to me because she was scared of all the crazy, violent stuff her dad did. People are so COMPLICATED.

'Will your granny come and live with you?' Joe asks.

My mouth falls open.

'OH MY GOODNESS! I hadn't thought about that,' I say. 'What if she has to stay for…well… ALWAYS?'

Joe frowns, like I'm missing the point.

'Yeah, OK, it wouldn't be great for you,' he agrees, 'but what about your granny? She needs help.'

I can tell he thinks I'm completely selfish so I nod

quickly, like I agree that my granny's needs must come first and I say, 'Yes, you're right.' But inside I'm panic-stricken. The idea that GT might move into the new flat with us FOREVER is a whole new enormous slice of WORRY PIE.

I distract myself from this by remembering that I have decided that today is the day that Fiona and I will have a dialogue and make friends again.

All morning, I keep looking out for opportunities to catch her on her own but Fiona talks to lots of other girls – Becky, Alice, even Samantha the miserable Goth. I don't get a chance to catch her without being heard by someone else and it's really upsetting to see her looking normal and happy without me. Doesn't she miss me AT ALL?

By lunchtime all the energy and hope that Dru gave me has trickled away and things feel bleak again. I eat my sandwiches outside the Art room ON MY OWN, while I wait for Mrs Allen. I need her help with some things for the zombie costumes. It's very quiet here and the quietness makes me feel even lonelier.

I am just thinking that this must be the quietest part of whole school at lunchtime when I hear footsteps. They are slightly uneven and each step is followed by the *tick-tick* of a walking stick tapping the ground. I hide my sandwiches because we're not supposed to eat in the corridors. A moment later a man comes around the corner, limping slightly. He is wearing a dark green suit (very smart) and has a scar on his left cheekbone. Suddenly, Mrs Crowther-Dupont bursts out of a door in front of him, flapping and blushing and acting all silly.

'Oh, Mr Finnegan, there you are!' she says.

So THAT'S the mysterious Mr Finnegan, and it's TRUE, he does have a limp and a scar, and Mrs Crowther–Dupont clearly fancies him like MAD. It's embarrassing to watch as she asks him, 'I wonder if you could help me with an article I'm reading about French wines' – she *whhiiines* – 'I know you're something of an expert.'

Fiona should be here to share this moment with me. She should be here to see Mr Finnegan sigh and smile patiently, and say, 'Certainly,' then follow Mrs Crowther–Dupont into the classroom. Fiona would understand why this is HILARIOUS and AWFUL at the same time. She would be as excited as I am about seeing the mysterious Mr Finnegan. Fiona understands me. Oh dear! I miss her SO MUCH.

Thankfully, Mrs Allen comes along to take my mind off my glumness. She digs around in her store cupboard and finds me some sludgy green fabric paint.

'Thank you, that's a good colour,' I say. 'But I still need a muddy brown as well, so that the waiters look like they've been buried for a while.'

'Try soaking the fabric in tea or coffee,' she suggests.

My eyes light up. This is a BRILLIANT idea. I'll get working on that ASAP. This weekend will be mad busy because on Monday I'm meeting the older kids who will be wearing my costumes, so I have to have something to show them. It's best to keep busy when you're feeling ABANDONED and MISERABLE.

As soon as I get to our registration group in the afternoon Jamila comes over.

'He apologised!' she says, looking surprised. 'Peter actually apologised to Aled and me about yesterday.'

HOORAY! I'm SO relieved that my plan worked. This means that the restyling of Peter's wardrobe can go ahead, but I don't mention this to Jamila, just in case she thinks I'm being too friendly with him. All I say to her is, 'Good. At least that shows he's HALF human.'

This news helps me to survive Geography. I sit on my own AGAIN and try to understand what Mrs O'Donnell is saying but I find it quite hard to concentrate. Geography isn't my best subject, and it's made EXTRA baffling today because I am distracted by Fiona, who looks like she understands EVERYTHING and is explaining it to Becky, when she should be explaining it to ME.

Peter comes up to me quietly and looking a TINY bit embarrassed at afternoon break.

'So, I did what you asked,' he says. 'I sorted things out with Jamila and Aled.'

'Good,' I say, not smiling too much but just enough to show that I approve. 'That means our shopping trip can go ahead, if you're still interested. How about Saturday?'

'Saturday's fine,' he says. 'I'll text you.'

'No,' I tell him. 'I'll text you and tell you where to meet me.'

He smiles, saying, 'OK, you're the boss.'

And I want to say, 'Yes, I am the boss but that doesn't mean I'm actually BOSSY,' but he's already gone into the next lesson so I don't get the chance.

It's good that he apologised. I'm beginning to think that, deep down, Peter Pompous Pants might be quite nice SOMETIMES.

I don't get a single opportunity to catch Fiona and have a dialogue and I don't want to report to Dru that I've failed, so I decide to give up for today and try harder tomorrow so that I can finally report some good news to the USA – that's IF it all goes well.

When I get home Mum and Dad are having a cup of tea and talking about Granny while they put leaflets advertising the Jug and Monkey into bundles. I sit down at the table and help myself to a home-made scone from a big warm plateful that Dad has put out. They both give me a little wave without looking up from their papers and their conversation.

'Did Dr Andrews come?' Dad asks Mum.

Mum nods. 'But Granny just hid in the cellar and shouted, "Air raid!" She thought she was back in London during the war again.'

'What did the doctor say?' he asks.

'She's going to send someone to do an assessment,' Mum explains. 'A specialist nurse who looks after the people at Goldenboughs. She'll do some blood tests and then we'll have to take her to the hospital for a scan.'

I look from Mum to Dad to see if I can tell what they're thinking, but I can't. Goldenboughs is an old people's home just up the road. The people in there are all a bit confused and need help getting washed. Mum and Dad both look sad. Mum has tears in her eyes again. Dad pats her hand and gives it a gentle squeeze. I don't really understand what's going on but I stop buttering my scone and give Mum a cuddle because she obviously needs one and SO DO I.

At dinnertime – bangers and mash, hooray! – my thoughts about how to get Fiona alone long enough to talk to her, and about zombie costumes, and Peter's wardrobe makeover are all interrupted by GT. I stare at her as she comes into the kitchen – we ALL stare at her. She has brought a brown paper bag with her and starts spooning mashed potatoes into it, saying, 'I might be peckish later and they don't sell sandwiches at the factory.'

Mum and Dad look at each other.

'What's she doing, Mum?' I whisper.

Mum touches my hand. 'Don't worry. She thinks she's getting ready for work at the car factory. She worked there as a typist for years when she was young. She's remembering things.'

'Is this another kind of time slip?' I ask.

Mum nods.

'What year is she in?'

'Somewhere in the 1950s,' Mum whispers. 'She's got muddled up again. It's a bit like when you rewind films so that you can watch certain bits over and over again but Granny doesn't have any control over which bits her brain will choose to replay.'

'And did typists used to eat mashed potatoes out of paper bags in the fifties?' I ask, frowning.

'No,' Mum says.

'So the mashed potatoes are just random?' I ask.

'Not in Granny's mind,' Mum explains. 'To her it makes sense.'

Then she tells GT, 'I've got time to pack you some sandwiches.'

'Are you sure? You've got a lot to do,' says GT, sounding polite for a change.

'I can help,' I say, joining in and hoping I can do something useful.

'Oh no, Deirdre,' she says to me, frowning. 'Your sandwiches are *terrible*. Let Mum do it.'

And she wanders off, away from the dinner table, carrying her paper bag full of mashed potatoes. Dad jumps up and catches a handful of mash as it drops through the bottom of the soggy bag. Most of it hits the floor with a heavy SPLOP. GT doesn't notice. She wanders off with the remains of the wet paper bag dangling from her hand.

Dad sighs and starts clearing up. Mum looks like she doesn't know whether to laugh about all this or burst into tears.

'We've got to keep our sense of humour,' she tells Dad, 'or we'll never cope with her.'

I am trying to put the puzzle together.

'So,' I say, with my finger in the air to get their attention, 'GT thinks you're **her** mum and she thinks **I'm** her sister, Deirdre, and she thinks that she still works as a typist at a car factory.'

'Sometimes,' says Dad.

'So who does she think **you** are, Dad?'

'Yesterday I was a bus conductor called Malcolm,' he tells me. 'I think she used to see him on the way to the factory, but today I'm just myself again and she's not speaking to me, so that's normal.'

Dad has finished scraping mashed potatoes off the floor. He washes his hands and comes back to the dinner table.

'What will happen to GT?' I ask.

Mum sighs again. 'Well, we'll need to look after her for as long as we can but if she gets very poorly and needs a nurse, she may have to stay in a nursing home.'

'Like Goldenboughs?'

'Yes,' says Mum, 'although it's very expensive so I don't think we can afford to keep her somewhere as nice as that.'

Dad ruffles my hair (I WISH he wouldn't, I'm not a puppy). 'You don't need to worry about all that stuff, Coco,' he says. 'That's for Mum and me to sort out. You just have to be patient and try not to mind about her being a bit mixed-up and needing your bedroom.'

When my parents explain stuff properly like this I don't mind things so much. And I have an idea.

'Did GT used to type on an old-fashioned typewriter like the one in the shed?' I ask.

'Yes,' says Mum, 'just like that one. She was pretty fast, too.'

'Why don't we get it out,' I suggest, 'and see if she'd like to use it?'

Mum and Dad look at each other.

'Excellent idea, Coco,' says Dad.

'Fantastic!' says Mum.

Dad and I hurry off to find the typewriter. I spot it first, zipped inside a grey case, stacked on a shelf in one of the old brick storage sheds in our big back yard. Dad pulls it out from behind the giant cans of olive oil we'll need for the restaurant and we bring it into the cottage where he sets it up on the kitchen table. That evening he spends AGES cleaning and repairing it so that it's ready to show GT in the morning. Mum and I are so interested in watching him do this that we forget to check on her.

'I'll find her,' I tell Mum. This gives me a good reason to peek into MY bedroom to make sure that GT hasn't wrecked my stuff.

I have a bad feeling as I climb the stairs, and, when I knock gently on MY bedroom door and peek in, I can't believe my eyes. GT is sitting on the bed holding my GENUINE 1950s evening bag that used to belong to Auntie Deirdre, and she's stuffing it full of chocolate biscuits! My mouth falls open and I gasp. GT looks up at me, and asks, 'May I borrow your bag, Deirdre? It's ever so nice,' and she strokes the velvety outside of it, like it's a cat.

There's no point getting cross. She is obviously far away on Planet Gran, so I take a deep breath and play along, even though I'm FUMING with her.

'Yes, of course you can borrow it,' I say, 'but let me get you a box for the biscuits.'

Then I back out of MY bedroom quietly and run downstairs to fetch Mum.

Mum eventually gets GT safely off to bed and I brush the crumbs out of my vintage evening bag and put it in the spare room under a pile of sewing fabric. Hopefully, GT won't find it there. Mum thinks she will have forgotten all about it in the morning.

That night, the imaginary air raid wakes GT up again with its bombs and we take her back to bed at 03.21. Her scary torch face doesn't bother me so much this time and I manage to go straight back to sleep once she is tucked up again. What a WEIRD life I lead.

8

The next day at school I STILL don't get a chance to speak to Fiona. She's ALWAYS with other girls. I don't seem to attract new friends, like she does. No one seems to want to be MY new best friend but Fiona has a queue of girls wanting to be hers. Perhaps I'm not as interesting as she is, or maybe I'm just not a very nice person. Now I'm having one of those I HATE MYSELF days. Nobody asks me why Fiona and I aren't hanging out together. Why would they? I'm obviously too boring to bother about.

As soon as I've finished my lonely-girl sandwich at lunchtime I peek into the rehearsal for the Halloween Cabaret. Fiona is up on the stage trying to rehearse. OH DEAR! I knew it would be a disaster with Ruby and Becky. The pair of them don't get through a single song without accusing each other of singing flat or being out of tune or of pushing in front, or being too loud. It's like watching

Cinderella's two ugly sisters having a fight – NOT very dignified.

Fiona steps back and doesn't get involved. Good for her. Mr Gampy tries to get Ruby and Becky to calm down and start again, but it's HOPELESS and he eventually tells them to come back tomorrow lunchtime 'with a different attitude'.

I hang around the hall for a while, hoping that Fiona will be on her own for a few micro-moments at the end of the rehearsal. She isn't. Becky comes back and sticks to her like a piece of old chewing gum. Did I see Fiona glance my way as they left the hall? I THINK I did but I can't be sure, and I'm still not brave enough to go up to her when Becky's around. It's Friday and there won't be another chance to talk to her until after the weekend. My heart feels like a crumbling biscuit. Why don't I just text her? No, no, no, Cordelia. Becky might see my text. Maybe I could send an email? No, Fiona might not read it. I could call, but Becky might hear, so that's no good. This needs to be a face-to-face dialogue, anyway, it HAS to be a proper chat. That's what friends do: they have proper chats sitting in the same room or in places like Bessie's Bakery. And they eat cake together. Will Fiona and I EVER eat cake together again?

♥

Granny Twigg is tapping away on the typewriter when I get home. I hear the **CLICK CLACK CLACK CLACKETY CLUNK** as soon as I step through the door. She is concentrating very hard, sitting at a little table in the corner of our tiny kitchen while Mum goes through piles of paperwork for Heckaby Picture Palace.

Mum raises her finger to her lips when she sees me, then whispers, 'Shhh. It's been lovely and peaceful here today,' and points to GT, who is oblivious to anything going on around her. Sheets and sheets of paper have floated down around her slippers. I peek at one of them from a distance, so that I don't disturb her. It says:

```
TO WHOM IT MAY CONCERN
OAUWR ;AR E A;SIRVA WRN X AWOIR;A
CAC;OIVF U OILJAR Ikla;oiro
aia948698918 eifja ravvadhoia as
```

```
vsghfoaaf afhfo;fkaf ;aroehah;oj\
Acjf;oijasjfcfc;oa fggdga as
Aac;I;ajdf;lfcmgy;
ire2s87g2sv7v7g444 a
Yours faithfully
```

I look at Mum and frown. She shrugs and whispers, 'She's happy, let's not spoil it.'

'What are we going to do with her?' I whisper back, glancing sideways, in case GT hears me.

Mum raises her finger to her lips again and looks over to GT. I suppose it's bad manners to talk about people who are in the same room, even if their brain is in another time-space dimension.

Dinner is one of Dad's scromlettes. These are great comfort food. It's like a big omelette but half scrambled with lots of onions, garlic, herbs and vegetables thrown in, and a thick sprinkle of melted cheese on top. The smells give you a warm and cosy feeling. A scromlette fills your tummy right up to the top and makes you sleepy.

GT seems almost normal again at dinnertime –

normal enough to be unkind about Heckaby Picture Palace.

Mum tells Dad that she's quite pleased with how the building is going but GT chips in with, 'Who wants to watch films in an old barn when they can go to one of those bright new cinemas with ten screens and a proper car park?'

Mum chews her scromlette slowly and swallows before she replies. She is SO good at thinking before she speaks. I wish I could learn to do that.

'Not everyone likes those places, Mum,' she explains calmly. 'And they don't have the sort of films that I want to show.'

I know she's my granny but I want to tell GT to go away and feed herself AND her cardigans to hungry vultures. Right at this very moment I don't care if she IS getting a bit old and confused, she's trying to stamp her feet all over my mum's big dreams and that's a HORRID thing to do.

'Tell her, Mum!' I say. 'Tell her about the sort of films you're going to show.'

I want Mum to talk about Laurel and Hardy and Charlie Chaplin, who were really funny, and about old, black-and-white monster movies like *Son of Frankenstein* and *The Old, Dark House* that aren't scary at all but are still brilliant. I want Mum to tell GT about the big, soppy, romantic films and the Westerns and all the films I know she can't wait to show to the children and old people who live around here. I've watched LOADS of them and I know Mum is right, people WILL enjoy them.

But Mum looks at me softly and says. 'It's OK, Coco. Granny can have her opinion.'

GT sniffs. 'You've got inflated ideas about yourself, girl,' she says to Mum. 'You don't really think anyone will bother to come all the way out here just to see a film, do you?'

Mum is SO patient, but I'm not.

'Mum isn't a girl, Granny,' I say, without shouting, which takes a LOT of effort because inside my head I want to scream. Instead, I point out firmly and clearly, 'She's a grown-up lady and she knows what she's doing.'

GT just sniffs again and looks at her plate. That's when my temper starts to bubble.

'People WILL come,' I say. 'All the kids at school are talking about it.' (That's not QUITE true but I want to stand up for Mum.) 'They'll come and bring their little brothers and sisters and their mums and dads.' I should stop my mouth right there but I don't, I let it keep motoring on and say, 'And their grandparents will come too…unless they're horrid and mean, like you.'

Mum and Dad both say, 'That's enough, Coco!'

GT just stares at me and says, 'Temper, temper, Deirdre.'

Good grief! She's gone weird again.

By the time Mum and I go down for breakfast on Saturday morning GT is already sitting at the table. She has about twenty-five hard-boiled eggs on a plate in front of her and is peeling the shell off one of them. Six more are bubbling in a pan of water on the cooker.

'Why don't you go on the computer for a little while, Coco,' Mum suggests, calmly. 'I'll find out what Gran is planning to do with all these eggs.'

I'm NEVER allowed on the computer before breakfast so she must REALLY want me out of the way for a while. I would almost prefer to stay in the kitchen and hear what GT says about the eggs, but I decide that a chance to use the computer this early in the morning is too good to miss. Dru has written back.

★ **Dru** to Cordelia

Hi!

You went offline before I had chance to tell you…We have a puppy! Here's a photo. Isn't he cuuuuuute? We can't agree on what to call him. Any suggestions?

She has attached a photo of a very curly-haired black puppy. He has black eyes, too, and a floppy fringe and velvety looking ears.

★ **Cordelia** to Dru

He is indeed a cutie. I'm **SO** jealous. Here's a way to choose a name that you can try:

1. Everyone in the family writes down their three BEST names.
2. Read out the names and everyone votes on each of them. If more than one person votes for the name, it goes into a sorting box.
3. You can vote for as many names as you like.
4. When the voting is done, get someone to pick one out of the sorting box at random.

★ **Dru** to Cordelia

```
   That sounds fair. I'm going to
suggest that. How are things going
with Fiona?
```

I admit to her that I've TEMPORARILY failed, then promise:

I'm going to keep trying. I won't give up. This is **TOO IMPORTANT**...and I have a tiny glimmer of good news in another area of my complicated life.

I tell her about Peter apologising to Jamila and Aled.

So the Peter Pompous Pants Project (PPPP) is going ahead!

That reminds me, I MUST text him and tell him where to meet me. Finally, I ask:

How is your Aunt Zillah doing?

★ **Dru** to Cordelia

```
   Aunt Z has her operation tomorrow,
```

so send big waves of love her way,
please.

Great news about the PPPP. Send
pics of how you transform this
INTERESTING but annoying boy.

I'm so glad you're not giving up on
Fiona. I bet she's just as sad as you
are.

I have to take No-Name Puppy out
for a puppy-poo now or there'll be a
stinky mess on the floor and I'll be
the one who has to clean it.

Love you!

Dru

xx

Back in the kitchen all the eggs have gone and so
has Gran.

'Where's GT?' I ask Mum.

Mum sighs. 'She's in the living room waiting
for the bus to the car factory. I've given her some
magazines to read so I think she's fine.'

'And the eggs?' I ask

'In a suitcase.'

'Of course!' I say, shrugging my shoulders.

'Where else would you keep thirty hard-boiled eggs?'

Mum and I smile about this. She's right, we have to see the funny side of GTs behaviour or we'll ALL end up a bit dotty with the stress. Dad comes in just then and sniffs the air, saying, 'It's a bit eggy in here, shall I open the window?

And Mum and I burst into giggles.

At breakfast I tell Mum about my plan to meet up with Peter this morning.

'So you'll be needing some money for bus fare and a cuppa, I suppose,' she says.

I give her a little smile and say, 'Yes, please.'

'Keep your phone with you,' she says, pulling a ten-pound note out of her purse. 'And keep it switched on.'

9

I text Peter:

> Cn u mt me @ th bs stn @ 11?
> C

He gets back to me straight away.

> Hi! I thought you'd forgotten our date.
> Yep, no problem. See you there at 11.
> I'm in town already. Peter.

Two things about this are annoying:

a) He texts in full sentences, like my dad.

b) We do NOT have a date, we have an appointment.

I won't mention this to Peter because there's no point – he would just get extra pompous and argue with me, then we'd fall out and I wouldn't get to organise his wardrobe, which would be even MORE annoying than the things he does and says.

Peter is waiting at the bus station when I arrive in Wellminster. We have an awkward moment when neither of us knows whether we should kiss on the cheek, do an 'air kiss', not touch each other or WHAT we should do. So we both just fidget and say, 'Hi.'

There are three charity shops in Wellminster that I like rummaging in (Dru calls them thrift stores, which I think is a better name for them). There's also a vintage shop that Fiona showed me called Pennyfeathers, which is quite trendy for such a boring town. I take Peter in there.

He looks a bit lost and puzzled when we step inside. I don't think Peter goes in shops very often and a vintage shop, where things are a bit jumbled up and you have to have 'creative eyes' like me, is probably completely baffling to him. I keep it simple.

'OK, what's your budget?' I ask.

My eyebrows go up in delight when he says, 'I've

got seventy-five quid,' because that's quite a lot of money to me.

'That should get us started,' I tell him. 'Just follow me, and do EXACTLY as I say.'

I know you're probably thinking, *What a bossy madam!*, but I am just being confident and taking charge of the situation. Anyway, he doesn't complain, so I carry on.

I pull things off the rail and hold them up to Peter. He looks down and mostly frowns and shakes his head with a begging look on his face, as if he's saying, 'Please don't make me try that on.'

I ignore this but he draws the line when I suggest he tries a tweed jacket with an orange flowery shirt underneath.

'Can I just point out,' he says, 'that this isn't a costume for prancing around on a stage. These are my actual, real, everyday clothes that we are shopping for. I have to walk around and catch the bus in these clothes, so they have to be comfy and not make me feel a complete turkey.'

I nod. 'OK,' I say, but my face clearly shows my disappointment in his fear of fashion adventures.

'I appreciate your enthusiasm,' he says, 'but shirts like that are a big *no*.'

'I admit it's a brave choice,' I say, using my most confident 'fashion adviser' sort of voice, 'but nothing in fashion is a NO, Peter, if you know how to wear it.'

However, I put the shirt back and look for something less orange. Eventually I send him to the changing rooms with some old Levis, some colourful shirts (no orange flowers) and a couple of waistcoats, because skinny boys look good in waistcoats.

After I have sent him back to the changing room another three or four times I feel that we are getting somewhere.

'Can we stop now?' he asks.

'Stop?' I say, feeling alarmed. 'But we're just getting started!'

He sighs and goes back into the changing room with a velvet jacket I've found and some different jeans. The jeans look particularly good on him because they're not too narrow and not too baggy – just right.

After a couple more trips to the changing room he is starting to look like he needs a cup of tea and a biscuit or he might fall over. We agree on the not-too-baggy jeans, a plain green shirt and a dark brown leather jacket.

He puts them on one more time and looks in the mirror. I am a little bit worried that he's going to change his mind. I'm biting my bottom lip. He takes a good long look at himself from all angles, and then nods.

'OK,' he says, 'they feel all right. What kind of trainers can I wear with this lot?'

I make a few suggestions and he nods again.

'But then there's your hair,' I say, because I have GOT to mention his hair.

He touches his head and screws his face up, saying, 'I'm not putting gel in it or anything else gloopy.'

He lets me move his hair about a bit with my fingertips, which is quite surprising because I don't imagine many boys would let a girl do this. I am VERY impressed with his patience. It NEARLY makes up for his pomposity.

'You've got great hair,' I tell him, 'it just needs a bit of what I call "joojing".'

'OK, but don't "jooj" too much,' he says.

When he looks in the mirror he has to agree that all I've done is let his hair go more or less the way nature wants it too, which gives him a nice floppy bit over his forehead.

Peter gives me a big fat NO again when I ask if I can take a photo – so that I can report to Dru.

'*No way!* I don't want my half-finished new image being splashed all over the internet, thank you.'

'I would NEVER do that,' I tell him, which is true. I would NEVER post a picture of someone else online if they didn't want me to. People who do that have frogspawn and vinegar for brains. Besides, I have NO online presence, remember?

We have a cup of tea in Bessie's Bakery and share a packet of chunky crisps. Luckily, we both like salt and vinegar flavour. Being in Bessie's should make me sad because we sit in the window where I usually sit with Fiona, but Peter is so chatty now that he's relaxed that I manage to put my sadness about Fiona to the back of my mind for a while.

I tell him about my granny going a bit fuzzy in the head and about Mum and Dad's plans for the Jug and Monkey and Heckaby Picture Palace, and how it is all CHAOS at the moment. But I don't moan about it – in fact we both laugh about my weird family life. Then he tells me something I wasn't expecting AT ALL.

'I'll be visiting my dad soon,' he tells me.

'Oh, where does he live?' I ask, expecting him to

say Leeds or Manchester or perhaps somewhere further away, like…I don't know…Belgium.

'He's in prison,' he tells me, watching my face very carefully to see how I take this MASSIVE news. Perhaps he's wondering if I will still want to be his friend? Well, fortunately, I know all about having a dad who lets you down BIG TIME. My dad didn't do anything illegal when he left Mum and me but he CERTAINLY did something stupid. So I feel like I can EMPATHISE with Peter and I just say, softly, 'Oh, that must be hard for you and your mum.'

I'm proud of myself for saying that because it sounds quite grown-up.

He nods. 'It's harder for Mum, of course. She's really cross with him because we lost our house and all our money. That's why I had to leave my other school.'

'Can I ask you what he did wrong?'

Peter takes a deep breath and says, 'He was an accountant for a big company and he stole some money from them.' He raises his eyebrows. 'A *lot* of money.'

'Wow!' I whisper. 'So it was some sort of clever computer crime?'

'Clever? Yes, he's clever,' says Peter. 'But not as clever as he thought he was, or he wouldn't have got caught, would he? That makes him *really stupid*. I don't think Mum will ever trust him again.'

I tell him that I know what it's like to have parents who aren't quite together and how you have to be patient with them because adults sometimes make the most ENORMOUS mistakes and we can get forgotten in all the muddle. I tell him how keeping focused on my big vision for the future – being **the ⁺⁺⁺ GREATEST ⁺⁺⁺ costume designer in the history of cinema** – makes the bumpy times, like right now, a lot easier to get through.

'What's your big vision?' I ask him.

He frowns. 'I don't think I have one.'

'Then I want you to think about it and tell me,' I say. 'I want you to think about what you would do if there was ABSOLUTELY NO POSSIBILITY that you would fail.'

He scratches his chin. 'Now *that* will give my brain something to work on,' he says, smiling.

'You've got until after the cabaret,' I tell him, 'then I'll ask you again.'

'OK,' he agrees, 'I'll get working on it.'

Then he changes the subject so that we both lighten up a bit.

'I'm getting some new glasses next week,' he tells me. 'What shape should I go for, d'you think?'

And, of course, I have plenty of advice. Peter not-so-Pompous Pants is really getting into his image transformation.

Time flies like a mad bat and I have to dash home. As I get off the bus I notice a big, yellow FOR SALE sign outside Driscoll's Discount. So, Mrs Driscoll really IS leaving? Hooray! She was so horrid to Joe in the summer holidays, accusing him of stealing from her shop and trying to get him in trouble with the police. None of the schoolchildren go near her place any more.

When I get home I find that GT has discovered Laurel and Hardy. She's watching a film where they try to get a piano up a very long flight of stairs and she's giggling like a toddler.

Mum comes in carrying a pile of papers.

'Gran seems happy,' I say.

Mum nods and grins saying, 'It's amazing…she

found a box of DVDs in your little room and she
hasn't moved from the television all afternoon.'

Alarm bells are ringing.

'Did you let her touch my things?' I ask,
frowning. 'She's already got my bedroom. I hope
she hasn't messed my stuff around.'

I dash upstairs to check.

Phew! No damage done, but there is
DEFINITELY a whiff of egginess. It doesn't take
long to find where it's coming from. Mr Belly is
under the chair, chewing a yolk into an eggy smush.
He has smeared it all over one of my lovely velvety
cushions – infuriating.

I take the smeary egg cushion downstairs and
show it to Mum. I am wearing my OUTRAGED
expression. This is when my lips go all tight and I
hold my breath.

'PLEASE can I have a lock on that door?' I say,
letting my breath out in a gush and waving the
cushion at her.

She takes it from me and sighs. 'Oh dear. Never
mind.'

Honestly! I spent hours sewing that cushion and
all my mum can say is *never mind*. There is NO
privacy in this house. I was in such a good mood

after my successful morning with Peter and now it's spoilt. I sulk through lunch. GT eats hers in front of Laurel and Hardy.

'You'd never let me eat MY lunch in front of the television,' I whisper to them in an angry way, as I tuck into my lasagne.

Dad rolls his eyes. 'You're not a dotty old lady, are you?' he says.

I suppose he has a point.

Straight after lunch I have to snap out of my bad mood and get to work *á toute vitesse* (ah-toot-vitt-ess) – AT FULL SPEED – on my zombie costumes.

I need some space to do this so I go down to the cellar under the pub and put on all the lights. This is where the beer barrels and the bottles of wine are kept. They are delivered through a hatch in the pavement outside and rolled down big planks. Dad also stores big boxes of tea and coffee on the old stone shelves down here. I'm going to take Mrs Allen's advice and use some of them to dye my zombie tops. I read the labels as I look for the strongest-looking one.

Lapsang Souchong

Earl Grey

English Breakfast

Formosa Oolong

Assam

Green Tea

White Tea

Rooibos

Chamomile flowers

The names of the different coffees make me want to travel around the world. Dad has big packets from:

- Tanzania
- Guatemala
- Ivory Coast
- Colombia
- Kenya

and:

- Costa Rica

I could get into a bit of a daydream about all these places, wondering if I'll ever get to visit them, but I'm down in the cellar to get on with zombie costumes, so I mustn't be distracted.

There are hot and cold water taps down here and lots of space. It makes a really good workshop.

I sort through the tea and coffee and choose the strongest-looking brands.

Perhaps I should ask Dad first but he's locked away in his kitchen doing food experiments and Mum says he is NOT to be disturbed, which is her way of saying, 'Don't go in there because he's in a bad mood.'

Mum has given me a pile of Dad's old vests – they'll make perfect zombie tops. However, they need a bit of design work so I've collected some big scissors, a wooden spoon, a washing line, a bag of clothes pegs and a bucket with a lid that has something in that I can't tell you about yet.

Using the scissors I cut slashes across the back and front of the vests and then fill six big plastic bowls with warm water. I sprinkle extra-strong-looking tea leaves into three of them and super-dark coffee into the others. I give each bowl a good stir with the wooden spoon to dissolve the mixture. You might wonder why we have so many plastic bowls. Well, we had to buy LOADS when we moved in here because the roof leaked and we needed them to catch the drips.

Next, I put the washing line up across the cellar. There are some very handy old nails in the walls that I can tie it to. Then I put two vests into each bowl and give them a poke and another stir with the wooden spoon until I can see that they're soaking up the colours of the tea and coffee – a good sludgy brown-grey. I'm not going to worry about tea leaves and coffee grounds sticking to them – it will make them look like they've been buried under the soil for a while before they jumped up zombie-style to chase people around and bite them.

The next part of the process is embarrassing and a bit disgusting and you must NEVER tell anyone about it or I will DIE of SHAME and then come back to haunt you for the rest of your life. I've read on the internet that before we had modern chemicals people used wee to make the dye stay in their clothes. HONESTLY, it's true. Look it up on a computer if you don't believe me. Anyway, I don't have any modern chemicals, so I have made a great sacrifice for the art of costume design and done a big wee in the bucket. I'm keeping the lid on tight, just in case anyone comes down here. If anyone finds my wee in a bucket in the cellar, my life would be OVER. I would have to go and live on a desert island or become a hermit and never go out into the world again.

But don't worry, I'll wash all the zombie tops before anyone wears them – just in case you are going, 'EUGH! YUCK! CORDELIA! HOW COULD YOU?'

It's all for the sake of my ART.

I hang all the vests on the washing line with the bottom hems still dangling in the coffee/tea bowls. This way the liquid keeps soaking in and up the vests and the tea and coffee stains will be darker at the bottom than at the top. I'm just about to tip the wee in when, DRAT-O-MATIC! Mum calls me.

'I need you to come to the supermarket with me, Coco!'

I hide the bucket of wee under a shelf and run upstairs.

Oh my goodness! We have just got back from a trip
to the supermarket and I am TRAUMATISED.

Granny came with us but we lost her somewhere
between the parsnips and the chocolate biscuits.
Mum and I had to split up to search the aisles. Mum
looked along BAKERY GOODS, SOUPS AND
TINNED VEG and BABY PRODUCTS while
I started at SOFT DRINKS and searched for her
through CRISPS, BISCUITS FOR CHEESE and
STATIONERY. Eventually, I spotted GT. She was
sitting in one of those big cage trolleys that they use
to move stuff around before putting it on the shelves.

'I'm sorry, Madam,' an assistant was saying. 'But
I'll 'ave to ask you to come out o' there.'

GT was huddled on top of a pile of toilet roll
multi-packs with her arms wrapped around her
knees. I found her at the same time as Mum,
who skidded in at high speed from the opposite
direction, still pushing our trolley.

'I'm not going until my mummy arrives. It's not safe,' GT was telling the man in her frightened little-girl voice – the voice that wakes us up at three in the morning.

He started to sound impatient. 'If I could just ask you to come out, please, Madam,' he repeated.

GT looked terrified and shook her head. 'Not budging!' she said. 'Not 'til Mummy comes.'

Then she looked up at him and shouted, 'You don't think Hitler's got her, do you?'

The shelf-filler man spotted Mum and me. We were just standing and staring at that moment because we couldn't believe what was happening. He looked VERY fed up and a bit cross with us. He looked back at GT saying, 'No, Madam. Hitler's bin dead a long time. He ain't gunna bovver no one no more. Now, outchya come.'

GT spotted us just then.

'Mum!' she called. 'I thought Hitler had got you.'

She unfolded herself and came out of the cage trolley but had left behind an EMBARRASSING LITTLE PUDDLE.

Mum was so glad that we hadn't lost GT completely that she didn't seem too worried about the puddle. She just said, 'Oh dear,' very calmly. 'You've had a little accident, Mum. We'd better get you home.'

Mum looked at the shelf-filler man and mouthed, 'I'm SO SORRY.'

I was scarlet with SHAME. I wanted to walk away and pretend I was someone else's child, but I knew that would be HORRID of me. I had to be brave and supportive and mature.

Mum whispered to the shelf filler, 'She's a bit confused.' But he didn't look very sympathetic. He just shook his head and shuffled away, pushing his cage trolley through two big doors.

Mum and I had to think very fast.

'Let's leave the shopping and take her home,' I said.

Mum nodded. What else could we do? As we passed the checkout I grabbed a couple of carrier bags off the pile. The girl on the till gave me a dirty look, like I was stealing the crown jewels, but I ignored her.

We sat GT on the carrier bags in the car and drove home quickly. Today seems to be all about weeing in the wrong place. It has to be fairly high on my top-ten list of strange days.

Mum has just helped GT to have a shower and put her to bed for a nap. She has sorted out Gran's clothes and they are whirring round in the washing machine. Now she's on the phone to the doctor's surgery.

I pop down to the cellar to check on my zombie tops but nearly jump out of my skin.

AAAAGH!

Two strange men are coming up the cellar steps. I am used to having workmen around because we have all this crazy building and decorating going on, but they don't usually appear from the depths of the cellar.

'It's OK,' Dad shouts from behind them. 'We're just looking at the plumbing. But come down here please, young lady, and explain something to me.'

Oh HORROR! He's found my bucket of wee! My dad and two complete strangers have seen my wee. I look down at my feet as the men pass me on the steps because I CAN'T make eye contact with someone who has seen THAT. I am frozen with fear and humiliation. They must be thinking I am some sort of SOCIOPATH – this is a good word.

It means a person with a personality problem who does EXTREMELY unacceptable things – I think leaving wee in a bucket in your own cellar counts as EXTREMELY unacceptable and my dad is about to tell me exactly that, probably in his most shouty voice.

But RELIEF-A-LLEUIA! It turns out that he hasn't found the bucket of shame, but is foaming furious that I've used some of his very expensive tea and coffee to dye old vests. Apparently, I've used about ninety-five pounds' worth. EEK!

Mum comes downstairs to see what he is exploding about and manages to distract him by saying, 'Can we deal with this later, John? I really need to talk to you about Mum.' And the serious look on her face makes him stop ranting on at me and follow her. DOUBLE-PHEW! If I stay out of his way for long enough, he might forget about the tea and coffee. I decide to tip the wee down the toilet and not bother with it. Having it around is too stressful – some experiments just have to be abandoned.

GT stays in bed for an hour then comes downstairs and does a bit more typing. She seems to have forgotten all about the supermarket incident.

After dinner, when she is back in bed, Mum finds a note that GT has left on her typewriter. She shows it to me and Dad and has a little cry about it.

```
Dear Sir/Madam
Thank you for looking after me.
I am very happy here.
Yours Sincerely
Mrs Nancy Twigg
```

Dad gives Mum a hug and Mum manages a little smile as she wipes her eyes.

'I'm visiting Goldenboughs tomorrow,' she tells him, 'to see if she might be more comfortable there.'

Dad nods.

I want to be involved in this conversation so I chip in with, 'I thought you said Goldenbough's was really expensive.'

Mum sighs.

'We might just have to use the money we've saved for the cinema,' she tells me. 'We have to do what's best for Gran.'

I gasp. 'But that's your big dream, Mum.'

'Sometimes our dreams have to wait a little while,' she says.

I don't want Mum to have to give up her dreams. That doesn't seem fair AT ALL. Why should GT, who has always been so horrid to her, use up all Mum's savings?

I lie in bed later, trying to think of a solution but there doesn't seem to be one, whichever way I look at the situation. This is one of those times where it would be very useful if I could do magic and just make everything work out right, but, as you know, THERE IS NO SUCH THING AS MAGIC in this world.

It is 03.27 when Hitler wakes GT up again. As Mum and I steer her gently back across the landing I step in something squishy. DRAT! EGGY SPLOT! I have to wash my right foot before I get back into bed so I am COMPLETELY WIDE AWAKE by the time I've dried it and got back into bed. I lie awake and worry about Fiona and our urgent need for

DIALOGUE, and whether my zombie costume idea will work and then Mr Belly jumps on the bed and starts doing a sort of egg-flavoured cat snore, so it's nearly 05.00 before I nod off again and I'm WRECKED in the morning.

♥

It's Sunday, and I go with Mum to visit Goldenboughs Nursing Home. GT comes along, too. She doesn't want to go anywhere without the typewriter today so I carry it for her in its zip-up case.

When we arrive we're met by a very friendly nurse in a smart blue uniform. Her name is Bonnie Matthews. She has a springy walk that makes her brown ponytail bounce as she leads us around, and a big, pretty smile. Mum has lots of questions for Bonnie who says that Granny can wander about freely and chat to people if she likes.

'I think she'd like to do some typing,' I say, holding up the case.

Bonnie says, 'No problem. Just find a space where she'll be comfy.'

'This is a nice office,' GT says, admiring the

big potted plants and the wide, sunny windows. 'Where's my desk, Deirdre?' she asks me.

'How about over there, away from the television?' I suggest.

She nods and we settle her down at a low table in the reception area. I make sure she has plenty of paper and is tapping away happily before I go back to Mum.

I find Mum just around the corner in a big, open sitting room full of completely ancient people. I don't mind old people. I'm not one of those girls who thinks that old folks are useless, but seeing lots of them together makes me feel a bit strange and I can't work out why…And there's a funny smell. Everywhere is lovely and clean and bright but there is definitely a bit of a whiff hanging in the air – a mixture of wee and disinfectant.

Some of the old people have visitors and are chatting away happily. They lean towards their visitors as if they want to get hold of them and not let them go, and their faces wobble a bit when they talk because of all the wrinkles and sagginess.

The people who haven't got visitors are mostly just watching space. Two of them are hunched over jigsaws and one is looking at a magazine but there are a lot of space-watchers, staring at nothing or at something they are imagining.

Mum is talking to a man who seems very pleased to see her. He looks about 200 years old. I've never seen such a crinkly face. When Mum asks him a question his face brightens up like a light bulb and he grins a big, happy, denture grin. You'd think that Ava Gardner or Ingrid Bergman, or another of those old-fashioned film stars, had just walked into the room wearing a sparkly evening dress and sat down next to him, but it's just my mum wearing her jeans. Mum introduces me. The man's name is Mr Phillips. I shake his hand, which is bony and freckled, and he gives me the big denture smile, too, but I don't think his eyesight is very good because he says, 'Nice to meet you, Christopher.'

I sit on a spare chair next to Mum. I can hear GT tapping on her typewriter around the corner, so I know she's OK.

'Mr Phillips used to work at the old cinema in Wellminster,' Mum tells me. 'Bonnie told him about our plans for Heckaby Picture Palace and he offered to show me some of his photos.'

'But…'

I start to say that there isn't going to BE a
Heckaby Picture Palace if GT comes to live here
but Mum gives me a stare and I know that I mustn't
say anything because it would spoil things for Mr
Phillips, who looks really excited about showing
Mum his photos.

Mr Phillips is sitting in an armchair and doesn't
move much except for his hands, which slide a pile
of faded photos around on a little white plastic table
in front of him. The table is on a stand with wheels
and it is pushed right under his chin. This way he
can see the photos better. He lifts each one up to
the end of his nose, then smiles as he recognises
something in the picture and tells Mum about it. He
has a lot to say but his voice isn't very strong, as if
his battery is fading.

'Of course, it's all gone now,' he says. 'They
knocked all the cinemas down in the seventies,
when everyone got tellies.'

Mum looks like she is under a spell. She frowns,
showing that she's concentrating on what he has
to say, and she only touches the photos if he passes
them to her.

'The Odeon became a bingo hall,' he tells her,
'then they flattened that to put a roundabout in,

then they made the roundabout bigger when they built the bypass. The Plaza was a better cinema. That's where I used to work. Lovely seats. Velvet curtains. Very posh, it was. But it was turned into an electricity showroom, where they used to sell cookers. That's been knocked down now as well. Beautiful building, it was. No one had ever been anywhere so grand as the Plaza.' He shakes his head. 'They built a tax office on top of it with a great big car park.'

Mum is listening as if he is passing on the SECRETS OF THE UNIVERSE. I think she's forgotten that I'm here. I look around but I'm still listening to them. Mr Phillips talks about 'the war' a lot.

'Of course, during the war the cinemas had to shut by ten o'clock. We had three in Wellminster. The Odeon, the Plaza and the Royal. Every town had at least two cinemas in those days. During the war it was difficult to get home. There were no street lights because of the blackout. We weren't allowed any lights at night in case the German bombers saw them.'

I think about GT waking up in the night expecting Hitler's bombs to fall. When very old people talk about their lives they often divide the things that happened to them into 'before the war', 'during the war' and 'after the war', or sometimes 'because of the war'. And when their memories get muddled they don't remember what order things happened in but they know that the 'the war' changed everything. It's like a big, dark crack running down the middle of their lives.

When Mr Phillips passes Mum the photos she looks at every millimetre of them, then hands them carefully to me and I hold them like they are priceless treasures. I spend a long time looking, too. I'm fascinated by the people's faces and clothes, and by the old-fashioned buses and cars passing in the streets. I put each photo back on Mr Phillip's table, very gently. They make me feel sad, somehow. Where have the glamorous, chatty people in those photographs gone? Where is their lipstick, where are their shiny shoes, the trimmings on their hats and their smiles? Have they ended up sitting in a nursing home, creaky and wrinkly and confused, hoping that they will have a visitor? Am I sad because they couldn't stay young and glamorous forever, or perhaps because the time when they were young has gone and can't ever come back again?

I leave Mum with Mr Phillips and go out through the patio doors to stand in the garden for a while, and THAT'S when I see…Becky Freemantle!

This is a VERY different Becky from the one who was fighting with Ruby at rehearsals and who is stealing my best friend. This Becky is tucking a blanket around an old lady in a wheelchair, smiling and chattering away happily. The old lady is chuckling, as if Becky were a little angel come to brighten up her day. Becky turns to walk back into the building. She can't avoid seeing me, and her face drops like a sack of potatoes.

'Hi,' she mumbles, not making eye contact with me. She only said 'hi' because she was taken by surprise, as if I'd caught her doing something that she didn't want anyone to know about. She's probably as shocked to see me as I am to see her.

'Hi,' I reply, in a blank way, not smiling.

What should I do NOW? Should I get angry with her for keeping Fiona away from me? I can't do that in front of all these people, can I? It's a very awkward situation and I don't feel like I can ignore her so I say, 'I didn't know you came here.'

She was just about to walk past me without answering but she changes her mind, stops and says, 'My mum's a nurse. She works here. I help out sometimes.'

'That's brave,' I say, 'but don't you find it all a bit sad and depressing?'

She frowns and curls her lip in a sneery way, like I've got the whole place totally wrong and must be as thick as two short planks.

'No,' she says very firmly. 'It's sad when they die, but that happens to everyone eventually, doesn't it? They have lots of interesting stuff to talk about.'

These are the most words Becky Freemantle has EVER spoken to me, and she hasn't finished yet.

'Just because they aren't dancing around doesn't mean they're unhappy,' she goes on. 'They just can't move very fast any more.'

I can see that she's right about this and I'm just starting to think that maybe Becky might be quite kind underneath her NASTY outside when she says, 'No wonder Fiona doesn't want to be your friend any more, you're obviously a bit stupid,' and walks off, stopping to smile and tuck a blanket around another delighted old person who thinks she's perfect.

Becky Freemantle clearly has more than one personality. This is weird and quite sinister…and I just don't believe what she says about Fiona.

Looking around again at all the ancient people here makes me think one day I'll be old, too, whether I like it or not. But I have SO much to do before then – I have so many costumes to make, so many places to visit, so many parties to go to. But the most important and urgent thing is that I do NOT want to grow old without making friends with Fiona. That would be truly tragic.

I report to Dru as soon as we get home. I tell her all about the supermarket trip and bumping into Becky at Goldenboughs, and how worried I am that Mum might give up on her BIG DREAM. I still can't give Dru any good news about Fiona but I make her a promise.

★ **Cordelia** to Dru

I **MUST** keep trying to have a dialogue with Fiona because it would be a tragedy if I end up in a nursing home when I'm 112 years old, missing her and wondering if she ever thinks of me.

...And have you given the puppy a name yet?

...And how did Aunt Zillah's operation go?

Love you!!!

Cxx

I spend the afternoon adding smears of Mrs Allen's green paint to the zombie tops and some smudges of coal dust from the cellar, then I hang them all near the old boiler to dry. I'm feeling very pleased with them so far.

Dad comes out of the pub kitchen after HOURS of experimenting and brings our dinner. He has made creamy garlic chicken with rice AND a blackberry and cinnamon crumble with vanilla custard – YUM!

GT has switched back to being unpleasant again.

'How's the building work going?' she asks Mum with her eyes narrow and hard. 'Have you given up your silly idea of opening a cinema?'

Honestly! Her brain is like a yo-yo springing back and forth, up and down, in and out of history and into different moods.

I know she can't help it but right now I want to

kick her under the table for what she's just said. My foot is twitching. I hear Dad breathe in sharply – a sign that, like me, he's trying to control his temper.

Mum doesn't get cross. She just pauses, turns away from us and pretends to be looking for something in the kitchen drawer, then she turns back and says, calmly, 'No, Mum, I'm a long way from giving up. Everything's going ahead. The inspectors came this week and they seem happy with the plans.'

GT has no idea that if Mum doesn't open her dream cinema it will be because she is kind and generous to GT, who does NOT deserve it. I want to tell GT the truth so that she'll feel ashamed. I want her to know what Mum is planning to do for her, to put her big vision on pause just so that GT can be looked after properly. But I CAN'T tell her, can I? It would just cause even more upset.

Mum brings the warm plates over, and Dad carves the chicken.

GT doesn't say 'thank you' when her delicious dinner is put in front of her. She just carries on being rude to Mum.

'And what do your neighbours think?' she says with her lips tight.

'Some of them don't like the building work,'
Mum explains. 'But we expected that.'

'I'm not surprised they don't like it,' GT snaps,
jumping on this idea and making it into something
much bigger than it really is. 'The noise, the extra
traffic, and when it's done there'll be problems with
parking and crime and hooliganism.'

Dad can't stop himself from chipping in at this
point. He's only trying to stick up for Mum. 'Why
would a cinema and a restaurant cause a rise in
crime?' he asks her, which is a perfectly sensible
question.

GT chews a mouthful of chicken, sniffs and pulls
her cardigan layers around herself more tightly.

'More people means more trouble,' she says.

'Not if they're nice people,' I reply.

GT ignores this.

'You'll be keeping the whole village up late,' she
goes on, and I am just about to explode and shout
at her when Mum gives me her '*don't you dare*' look,
the one where she raises her eyebrows and does
goggle-eyes at me, like she could shoot laser beams
out of them, so I have to keep quiet, which is the
hardest thing in the world when something SO
unfair is going on.

Later, GT watches the news in her dressing gown while I try to do some Geography homework. I sit with my back to the television so that I don't have to look at her and so that I'm not distracted.

It is 03.50 when Mum and I are woken up again by GT doing her Hitler routine.

When she is tucked up in bed again and we are shuffling back across the landing Mum says, 'You mustn't think that I mind about the cinema, Coco.'

I am too tired to reply but I know that she's just being brave and kind and it seems to me that I can almost hear her heart breaking at the thought of not opening her dream cinema. It's like the sound of a glass falling in slow, slow motion onto a hard stone floor.

GT is up early and boiling eggs again on Monday morning. She fills her cardigan pockets with them and then goes over to her little table and starts typing.

I don't speak to her. If I do I'll get angry so it's best if I stay quiet and eat my breakfast. Mum is upstairs having a shower and Dad hasn't come in from the caravan yet, so it's just the two of us in the tiny kitchen at the moment – not speaking.

I am spreading marmalade on my toast with my back to her when GT stops typing and starts to make a soft sniffling sound. I turn around to look and for a moment I have NO IDEA what to do because GT is CRYING.

'It's not fair,' she blurts out. 'It's not fair. You don't know anything about my life. You don't know anything about me.'

I think she's talking to me. I don't think she's in her time-slip world at the moment. I put down my toast and try to think what's best to do. I can hear the plumbing making noises – Mum must still be in the middle of her shower and won't be downstairs for a little while.

'What isn't fair?' I ask, gently, because I don't want her to shout at me.

'Not liking me and not speaking to me. It isn't fair.'

'I'm sorry,' I say. 'But you say very hurtful things to my mum and I don't like it.'

'I get muddled,' she says, 'and I get frightened.'

'But you've always said nasty things to her,' I point out. I might have gone too far but it has to be said. 'It isn't something that's started since you got muddled, is it?'

GT looks at me with watery eyes, her chin trembling. Is she going to shout? She doesn't reply straight away. I can't take back what I've said now. But instead of shouting she sighs, a long, slow sigh, and says, 'I'm sorry.'

She looks out of the window, blinks, as if she's trying to see something in the distance, then sighs again, repeating in a sad whisper, 'I get frightened.' Then, talking to someone invisible, or perhaps to me, it's hard to tell, she says, 'The bombs frighten me. You might not still have a mum and dad in the morning. Some children don't. I'm always scared.'

'But there isn't a war on now, Gran. Not here,' I tell her, speaking more softly and kindly now. She carries on staring out of the window at something far away, like she's trying to look into the past.

'I'm scared of the other girls at the factory, too. They tease me because I'm not pretty and I haven't got a boyfriend, and I can't dance very well.'

Her mind seems to be hopping between the different scary times in her life. Now she's remembering the car factory. As I'm listening I'm thinking that it's just the same at my school. People get picked on for the same sort of things. I try to imagine GT when she was a little girl, frightened by bombs. Then I see her when she was a bit older than me and going to work, being teased and bullied. Mum says that people who don't feel safe when they're young can become worriers, and worriers can be bossy and unfriendly. They can even become nasty bullies themselves. Could all GT's unfriendliness have started with being scared when she was little and then bullied when she grew up? I think it did. I think she let the bad things in her life turn her into a worrier and a bossy grumpster. It feels like a lot of time wasted and it makes me sad for her.

'You don't need to worry about all that any more, Gran,' I tell her. 'But don't take it out on Mum. It wasn't her fault that you were scared and you were teased. And she's got a big dream. Don't try to squash her. Don't try to make her frightened.'

A big tear drops off GT's cheek onto her wrinkly hand. Another one joins it and they roll down between her bony little fingers. She looks straight at me now and seems to be back in the present for a moment.

'I'm just scared for your mum, and for you,' she

says. 'That cinema idea. What if it goes wrong? You could be left with no money. I just want you both to be safe.'

'Honestly, Gran, you can stop stressing about us. Mum's really strong and brave, and so am I. And I know you don't think much of my dad but he loves us both ever so much and he works really hard. Everything's going to be all right for us.'

This is one of those moments that feel HUGE. It's one of those times when you know that what you do next is really important for the future. I could tell GT off. I could shout at her for being horrid to Mum. I could tell her that I HATE the things she says and I wish she wasn't here but THANKFULLY I don't do that. Thankfully, I can empathise with GT. I can see that, on the inside, she's just all mixed up – like I am sometimes.

'Try to be more kind to Mum and Dad,' I tell her, doing my best to sound like a nice teacher, or like my mum when she's being an angel. 'And try to be brave, then you won't be stressy and snappy.'

GT sniffs and I tear off a piece of kitchen towel from the roll on the table and hand it to her. She wipes her pale eyes with it. They are rimmed with pink and still misty with tears. I can't stop myself from giving her a hug. I've never done this before. I've never wanted to hug her before, but right now, I do. I am COMPLETELY shocked by what I'm doing, and amazed that Granny Twigg has actually said sorry.

She sniffs again and reaches into her cardigan pocket, then pulls out a handkerchief that she must have forgotten she had. A hard-boiled egg comes out with it and splats onto the floor.

'I'll tidy that,' I say. 'You just relax.'

I scrape up the egg. Mr Belly helps me by licking the floor tiles. Before I leave for school I give GT a kiss on her cheek. I never thought I'd do that.

'It's OK,' I tell her. 'We'll look after you.'

And it's strange, but I mean it. Just at this moment, I love my granny.

Then I call 'goodbye' to Mum, who is just on her way downstairs, and run for the bus, leaving GT to get on with her typing. She has already started again:

```
Dear Sir or Madam
I am writing to complain
about aoiwrcbiucfa oiaewr
apasknf5a;f7f98r;as'fpl,ac8af
```

```
,asf5a.aocfmjvhafaf55afackas;oj
Fkoarf fa ;a rja c
pkasrmcfhfy[pkaroijamko
```

Yet again, I can't get near Fiona before school. I drag myself off to Science. Peter catches up with me in the corridor.

'Thanks again for the wardrobe help,' he says.

'No problem,' I tell him, doing my best to sound like it was just an oh-so-tiny thing and that I restyle people every weekend.

'I've started throwing things out that I'll never wear again,' he tells me, 'and I've sorted what's left into piles of "maybe keeps" and "definitely keeps".'

'Wow. That's great. You're really getting organised.'

I hadn't expected him to take this restyling project so seriously. He starts describing a jacket that he doesn't know whether to keep or throw away but Ruby interrupts and blocks our path.

Now, if Ruby MacPherson sees you even TALKING to a boy she tells BIG FAT FIBS to everyone in your registration group like, 'I saw those two snogging,' or, 'I saw him touch her bottom,' or else she sticks a sheet of paper on the wall that says,

'Those two did...' with a long list of REALLY rude stuff that you NEVER even thought about doing so that you nearly DIE of embarrassment and don't dare speak to the boy again. Sometimes she just walks past when you're talking, and makes sloppy kiss noises with her lipsticky mouth just to WIND YOU UP. (We're not supposed to wear lipstick but the teachers seem to have given up telling Ruby off about it.)

I mostly manage to ignore her these days. You can't let that sort of STUPID behaviour stop you from making friends, can you? But it isn't easy to ignore her when she stands RIGHT in front of you on your way to a Science lesson.

'Kissy, kissy,' she says, and laughs in a nasty way, then puckers up her sticky pink lipstick at us – YUCK! – and walks away.

I am going SCARLET and I can feel my blood boiling. I MUST NOT shout at her. I MUST NOT lose my temper or Peter will think I'm a crazy girl who can't control herself. He doesn't seem bothered AT ALL by this very humiliating 'kissy' thing that she's just done.

I'm feeling MORTIFIED and full of HATRED for Ruby.

'She loves embarrassing people,' I tell him as soon as she's gone.

Peter laughs and just says, 'I'm not embarrassed about the idea of kissing you, Cordelia Codd.'

I go from scarlet to PURPLE with TERROR and hurry off to Science.

'Don't be silly,' I tell myself. 'He's Peter. He's Peter Pompous Pants. There's NO WAY he's going to kiss me.'

12

I try to get to Science quickly. My plan is to just sit down next to Fiona and not budge. Then I can pass her a note in the lesson arranging to have DIALOGUE. This seems safer than texting or trying to talk in front of Becky. I have the note ready:

Hi,
Please let's talk at afternoon break. Usual place.
C x

But Becky beats me to it. She is already sitting next to Fiona when I get there. She does the same in English, too, so I don't get a chance to pass Fiona my note and I'm LEMON SOLO – ON MY OWNIO all morning.

Becky keeps looking at Fiona's work and

distracting her. I bet Fiona doesn't like that. Why is she putting up with it? Why doesn't she just move back next to me?

OH! It's all so INFURIATING and CONFUSING.

Fortunately, I haven't time to worry and fret and get miserable about it for too long today because I'll be showing the costumes to the zombie waiters at lunchtime and my brain is busy with that. I'm pretty pleased with how the vests have turned out. They really do look like someone died and got buried in them.

Lunchtime seems to take ages to arrive but when I get to the Drama studio with my costumes I find that some of the big kids who are going to be waiters haven't even BOTHERED to turn up. There are supposed to be twelve of them but there are only eight here. Why are people so UNRELIABLE? It makes me FURIOUS. But those who do turn up are REALLY impressed when I show them the zombie tops.

They each try on a vest and we agree that they look PRETTY NASTY, which is exactly what I wanted. I ask them to find something for the bottom half of their costumes.

'It could be an old nightie or pyjama bottoms that you've rubbed a bit of mud into.'

They all agree to find something.

'And please remember,' I say quite loudly to make sure they've heard and understand, 'to make your hair look as BAD HAIR DAY as you possibly can. NO hair straightening and NO pretty make-up. You're supposed to be DEAD and scary.'

By the end of the day I STILL haven't managed to catch Fiona alone. Every day that we don't talk it seems as though Fiona is slipping further and further away from me. I can't POSSIBLY report back to Dru that I've failed AGAIN.

After school Mum picks me up in the car. I've promised to help her with another supermarket shopping trip because we had to abandon the last one after GT's LITTLE ACCIDENT.

'Where's Granny?' I ask her, remembering her tears at breakfast time and our little hug.

Mum glances sideways at me, like she isn't sure that she wants to answer my question.

'She's visiting a new friend,' Mum tells me. 'But I can't leave her for more than a couple of hours, in case she has a funny turn. I don't want Mrs Driscoll to have to cope with her when she's muddled.'

My mouth drops open. 'Mrs Driscoll! You're letting her hang out with Witchy Driscoll, the most miserable woman in the village, who hates us? Who hates EVERYBODY!'

No wonder Mum looked a bit worried about telling me.

'Granny is allowed to choose her own friends, Coco,' Mum insists.

'But the two of them together will be completely poisonous,' I tell her.

'I know Mrs Driscoll isn't exactly a bundle of fun,' Mum admits.

I get a bit shouty. 'She's a BASKET OF SNAKES.'

'They got chatting when I took Granny to the post office for a walk,' Mum explains. 'I'm sure it'll be OK, and it gives me a little break. I had quite a battle with her at the hospital this morning when we went for her tests.'

'I know you need a break from her,' I say, 'but

she'll come back even worse because Witchy Driscoll will tell her all sorts of lies and gossip.'

I can see what's going to happen. Just when GT is starting to be gentler and I'm doing so well at starting to like her, and we even had a little cuddle, Mrs Driscoll will stir things up with her poisonous tongue. Mum has NO IDEA how much damage this could do.

'Don't worry,' says Mum. 'Anyway, Mrs Driscoll is leaving Heckaby soon. She's sold the shop.'

Now THAT is good news, but it's come too late to stop Witchy Driscoll turning GT into a grump again.

'I hope she's going a LONG way away,' I say.

Mum tuts at me for being unkind.

'Well,' I say, 'she accused Joe of stealing from her shop. Have you forgotten? And she makes such a fuss about our building work. She just isn't friendly AT ALL. I'm glad she's going.'

Mum and I have to whizz around the supermarket extra-fast so that we can get back and pick GT up from Witchy Driscoll's before she has one of her 'peculiar episodes'.

♥

I refuse to go into Mrs Driscoll's shop to pick GT up. Mrs Driscoll has always been especially horrid to schoolchildren, so I wait in the car. I move into the back seat because it's easier for GT to get in the front with her walking stick.

'Did you have a nice time?' Mum asks her, smiling, as they get back into the car.

Here it comes, I think to myself. *I bet she's going to start blurting out all sorts of nasty gossip about us, and about everyone else in the village. Mrs Driscoll will have filled her full of FIBS.*

So you can imagine how MIND-BOGGLED I am when she gives a little huff and says, 'Well, I won't be going there again.'

Granny and Mrs Driscoll didn't get on! How come? I am desperate to know why, so I sit up and lean forward, trying not to look nosey.

After a short pause – because she is probably also MIND-BOGGLED – Mum says, 'Oh dear. Why's that? I thought you two were going to be good friends.'

'That woman is poisonous,' says GT.

I have to put my hand over my mouth to stop myself from laughing.

'Really?' says Mum, as if she didn't know. 'What was she saying?'

'She was very rude about you, Cordelia.' (I am Cordelia, not Deirdre, at the moment, clearly.)

'She says rude things about all schoolchildren,' I tell her.

'And she wasn't nice about that lovely young man who came round,' says GT.

GT remembers Joe? Maybe her memory isn't completely FURBLED after all.

'Oh, she doesn't like Joe,' I tell her. 'She accused him of stealing from her grotty little shop, but he's actually a hero. Did she tell you that he saved little Mina's life, the girl who lives at the newsagent's?'

'No, she didn't,' says GT, sounding like she wants to know more, so I tell her.

'Mina fell in the river when we had a flood and Joe jumped in and pulled her out. He had to go the hospital in a helicopter.'

'She didn't mention any of that,' says GT, being chattier than I have EVER known her before. 'She hadn't a good word to say about anyone and she seems to think that you lot are some sort of criminal family. So I put her straight on that.'

'Oh,' I say, trying to sound only mildly interested even though I am bursting to hear more. 'What did you say to her?'

Mum is concentrating on watching the road. I bet she can't believe what she's hearing. Granny Twigg is actually sticking up for us.

GT folds her arms over her cardigans.

'Well, I told her that she was *out of order* and that it was my family she was being rude about,' she begins. 'I said, "You're a proper sour lemon, aren't you? You need to sweeten up a bit or you'll die a lonely old lady and no one will care."'

I gasp.

'You were brave,' I tell her.

'Some things have to be said,' GT insists. 'She'll thank me for it in the long run. I think she's a bit wrong in the head myself.'

This is strange coming from an old lady who can also be a proper sour lemon and who is DEFINITELY showing signs of being 'a bit wrong in the head'.

'I wouldn't worry about her,' I tell GT. 'Everyone knows she's a meanie.'

Well, can you believe it? Here I am, chattering away with GT as if we were friends. I NEVER thought that would happen. It just shows that one little hug can change things around COMPLETELY.

Mum is quiet but I bet she's giggling inside. We're not used to having GT on our side. It's all a bit strange.

GT is still being nice at dinnertime. She even says 'thank you' to Dad for her chilli con carne and lemon meringue pie. Dad is a bit surprised. I'm a bit surprised. Mum is a bit surprised. Perhaps GT has surprised herself.

'It's like she's a different person,' I say to Mum and Dad when GT has been settled into bed.

'I hope it lasts,' says Mum, as she picks up the newspaper. It's a hard job getting GT to bed and she needs to relax.

'Why do you think she didn't make friends with Mrs Driscoll?' I ask as I help Dad to dry the last of the dishes. 'They're quite similar in some ways.'

'That'll be exactly why,' says Dad. 'It must have been like looking into a mirror and not liking what you see.'

Mum gives a little laugh. 'Yes, you could be right,' she says.

I look at Mum and then at Dad. It's nice to see them laughing and agreeing about something, and I think I know what Dad means, but I need to get it clear.

'So,' I say, frowning, 'you mean that she heard Mrs Driscoll being grumpy about everyone and realised that she sounds like that, too, so she decided to stop?'

Dad nods. 'It could be as simple as that,' he says. 'But she wouldn't admit it, of course. This way she can change without ever having to admit that she used to be a grumpy old thing.'

I hope this is true because then Mrs Driscoll will have done something useful for our family before she leaves, even if she doesn't realise it.

'Maybe,' says Mum, looking up from the newspaper, 'but Gran might be too muddled to DECIDE to change her behaviour. Perhaps the change happened deep inside her, without her even realising what was going on.'

Both of these explanations seem possible, but I'd like to think that my conversation with GT this morning helped, especially the hug at the end. I'd like to think that it was partly due to HUG POWER.

I don't get a chance to ask any more because GT wanders downstairs again and starts calling me Deirdre, and asking Mum where the plumber is (I think she means Dad, but I'm not sure).

'That man who was here for dinner,' says GT, 'has he fixed the toilet yet?'

'That was John, my husband,' says Mum. 'He's just popped into the other kitchen.'

GT laughs. 'Don't be silly, Mum,' she says, 'you're married to Dad.'

Because, of course, she thinks that my mum is HER mum and that my dad has just come to fix the plumbing. Oh well! I think we can cope with GT being strange, it's better than when she's being A PROPER SOUR LEMON.

Mum gets downstairs the next morning before GT has a chance to start boiling eggs. I am not far behind her. She is lining up bottles of tablets on the kitchen table.

'Are they all for GT?' I ask. 'Wow! How many does she take?'

Mum is counting so she ignores me at first.

'…Two…three…Monday…Tuesday… Wednesday…Four…five.'

When she pauses to put the little piles of tablets into a plastic box she says, 'I had no idea she was taking all this lot until I went to the hospital with her. She might have been forgetting to take them so I'm organising them into a pile for each day.'

'What are they all for?' I ask.

Mum points to the pink, then the green, then the orange tablets, saying, 'Heart, kidneys, blood pressure...and the yellow ones are to help her sleep.'

'Well, THEY'RE not working, are they?' I say, yawning.

I couldn't go back to sleep after GT had disturbed us AGAIN. When I eventually nodded off I had a nightmare about being chased through a supermarket by zombies waving toilet rolls.

Mum starts to make some coffee for her and Dad and puts some bread in the toaster.

'Granny is really very poorly,' Mum says. 'You understand that, don't you, Coco?' She says this in a soft voice. Grown-ups speak like this when they want to make sure you understand that something is serious. What Mum really wants to say is that GT might die soon but she doesn't want to say it directly in case it scares me.

I nod to show Mum that I understand because I don't want her to worry. There isn't time to talk about it properly because GT shuffles in just then and we both wait for her to say something, so that we can work out where her brain has travelled to this morning. Is she working in the office at the factory, or back in the Second World War, or here with us in the kitchen?

'Morning!' she calls as she bustles past us to her typewriter. She's fully dressed and carrying her handbag so it looks like she's back at her imaginary work today.

'Morning!' we reply. Then we wait. She settles at the typewriter and winds paper into it.

'Cup of tea, Mum?' My mum asks.

'Not until breaktime. We're not allowed drinks at our desks,' says GT and starts work on her latest letter.

'OK,' says Mum over the *tappety tap tap* of the keys. 'Just let me know when you're ready.'

'You'll hear the bell,' says GT, 'unless you're deaf. It reminds me of the old air-raid sirens. All that noise just to tell us we can have a cup of tea.'

'Who are you writing to this morning?' I ask.

'That's confidential, Deirdre. You know I can't always talk about my work.'

I turn to Mum, who passes me the butter and

marmalade, and I whisper, 'Did she used to do top secret typing work?'

Mum shakes her head and whispers, 'I've no idea.'

Becky isn't going to let me get near Fiona. I try to catch Fiona's eye but she is either too scared to look at me or doesn't want to. In History I try to send a telepathic message that I want to talk to her but it doesn't seem to get through.

At lunchtime I have another meeting with the zombie waiters. This time they ALL turn up and some of them have brought along old pyjama bottoms and nighties to wear with their zombie tops. Julie has brought some face paints to share and Debbie has some stick-on scabs. I put dabs of theatrical blood on the vests while they practise carrying the trays they will use for drinks and snacks. It's all going pretty well.

I hear the singers trying to rehearse again and I can't help stopping to watch. It's still a shambles. I can hear Ruby being horrid to Becky.

'You've got a voice like a cat with a sore throat,'

she says, with her hands on her hips, 'and you keep distracting me because you're wiggling too much.'

'Just start from the beginning again,' Jason tells them.

I can see that he's getting REALLY fed up. Fiona sits down and waits for Ruby to stop shouting at Becky, but Becky shouts back, 'Everyone knows you sing too loud, Ruby Big Mouth. We're all supposed to try and sing together, but you keep getting louder and louder until no one can hear anything else. It's *you* that's the problem, not me!'

Fiona is sitting on the edge of the stage sighing and swinging her legs. I bet she's having a terrible time. She must be bored stiff listening to those two. Eventually Jason walks away saying, 'I'm going to try my dress on, I haven't got time to listen to you two drama queens.'

Fiona isn't in school that afternoon. On the bus home I ask Joe if he's seen her as we share his packet of corn chips.

'Not since morning break,' he says. 'We were hanging out near the basketball pitch.'

'Was Becky there?' I ask.

'No, it was just the two of us.'

I make a note in my brain that if I want to catch Fiona for a dialogue I should look near the basketball pitch tomorrow breaktime. Joe won't mind if I want some time with her alone. He looks around the bus and narrows his eyes suspiciously.

'Hmm, I notice that Becky isn't on the bus tonight,' he says. 'D'you think they skipped school together?'

'What! Fiona? She'd NEVER skip lessons. She's not stupid.'

Joe doesn't sound so sure. 'Becky does it a lot. If Fiona is friends with her at the moment Becky might've pushed her into it.'

This is REALLY worrying. Fiona CAN'T miss school. She'll never be a pyrotechnic engineer if she starts doing stuff like that. I have to save her.

I tell Joe that I've been trying to catch her alone to have a dialogue but Becky is sticking to her like glue. I tell him about the disastrous rehearsal she was having today.

'She must be getting sick and tired of it by now,' he says. 'I bet she's missing you.'

'Then why doesn't she text me?

Joe shakes his head. 'Perhaps for the same reason you don't text her. Because she wants to talk properly.'

I hadn't thought of that.

13

When I get home Mum has been BRILLIANT. She has scored **five** stars by going to the joke shop in Wellminster and buying me some more fake blood and zombie face paints. She has also bought me a big rubber spider on a string, but Mr Belly jumps on that and starts batting it around the floor with his big strong paws. I say, 'Thank you,' and give Mum a big hug.

GT is having a nap and Dad is experimenting with something that smells of mint and lamb that is wafting in deliciously from the pub kitchen, so Mum and I have a cup of tea and I am just about to tell her about falling out with Fiona when there is a quiet knock at the door.

'I'll go,' I say, and dash off, but I nearly faint when I open the door to find Fiona herself standing there, all alone, sobbing and carrying a HUGE bar of chocolate. Her eyes are bright pink around the edges and her nose is like a tomato.

'You look like someone ran over your kitten!' is all I can think of to say.

'It's **worse** than that!' she says with a sniff. 'The whole cabaret is a **disaster.** Our singing sounds **terrible** and we all look **ridiculous**. You were right about Ruby and Becky, they've egos the size of Jupiter and tempers like Rottweilers. And Becky won't let me go anywhere near you. I've been trying to text you or pass you a note but she hovers around me like a big **vulture** all the time. She made me skip off school this afternoon and we got **caught**. It was **horrid**. And I **miss** you, you're so **normal** compared to her.'

I am SO pleased to hear her say, 'I miss you,' that I temporarily forget all the rest. My heart is beating fast, like when I've had too much sugar.

'It's really BORING without you,' I tell her and we have a big hug right there on the doorstep. 'I've been trying to talk to you, too, but I was scared of Becky. That was really COWARDLY of me. I'm SO sorry.'

'I'm scared of her, too,' says Fiona. 'But no more. I've stood up to her now, but I think she might be planning to **kill** me.'

I get her inside quickly and let Mum know that she's here.

'Lovely to see you, Fiona!' Mum calls. 'Are you sleeping over?'

'Not tonight, thank you, Mrs Codd,' Fiona calls back from the hall. I don't think she wants Mum to see her tomato nose. 'My mum's picking me up in an hour,' she explains. 'She's just gone to visit a friend.'

We run upstairs and huddle in the tiny spare room for an URGENT GIRL CONFERENCE. Just as we are getting down to our dialogue, GT walks past and calls to Fiona, 'Good morning, Mrs Cardew. I've nearly finished those letters for you, shall I leave them on your desk?'

Fiona looks at me and frowns, as if she has a big question mark in the air over her head.

I whisper, 'Just say "yes".'

'Yes, thank you. That would be lovely,' Fiona instantly replies.

GT gives a little smile and a nod and shuffles off quickly.

I explain that I have NO IDEA who Mrs Cardew is.

'She probably worked at a car factory with Gran once.'

Fiona knows that my family is a bit weird, so she just accepts this and we laugh about it.

Then we settle down on cushions, with Fiona's bar of chocolate, and she tells me about Becky making her miss school.

'She said I had to go with her, or she'd **push my head down the toilet and flush it,** but all we did was sit in the park all afternoon with a can of lemonade and some crisps. She smoked cigarettes and tried to make me smoke, too, so I did and it made me throw up in a flowerbed – I'm **never** doing that again. And it was cold outside. I was bored stiff and just wanted to be back at school. Then Mrs Allen walked past with a group of year seven kids looking for leaves to make prints with and she just said she'd "deal" with us tomorrow. It was so **humiliating**. I felt like such a **loser**.'

She breaks off another piece of chocolate for each of us and we chew in silence for a few seconds until I say, 'Becky will be a loser if she doesn't shape up, but you WON'T. You're going to be the world's most whizzy-bang pyrotechnic engineer!'

Then I ask her to tell me what on earth is going on with the rehearsals and she has to blow her nose before she can even start because she's SO upset, but then she blurts it all out at about one hundred miles an hour without stopping for breath.

'I thought Ruby and Becky would just get on with the singing,' she tells me, 'but they made it so **complicated** and **difficult** because of their arguments and Mr Gampy was very clear that all three of the backing singers should wear black, just plain black...but Ruby said afterwards that she didn't care what Mr Gampy wanted, she was going to wear her bright green dress with sparkly bits and he could **get lost** if he didn't like it. Becky and I didn't think she would **dare** but she wore it for the rehearsal yesterday and she looked like a massive, wiggling Christmas tree. Mr Gampy went crazy and told her to turn up on the night wearing black or else she would be out of the show, but then Becky told me that **she** wasn't wearing black if Ruby wasn't. She's planning to wear a pink and yellow dress with sequins – honestly! Sequins! It's a Halloween cabaret not a ballroom dancing competition! She said she wasn't being outdone by Ruby and that I'd better wear something that isn't black, too, so that we can all show Mr Gampy that he's not bossing us around and she said **again** that if I wear black *she's going to put my head down the toilet and flush it*. So I said I wasn't going to hang out with her any more because she's a bully but I think she means it about the toilet this time so now I'm **scared** but I **don't want to dress up like a Christmas tree!**'

And she has a big SOBATHON, which is unusual for Fiona because she's much tougher than me but it's a sign that she has been TRAUMATISED.

'OK,' I say, 'lets stay calm and consider the options.' I get a notebook and write them down.

a. Wear your black dress anyway and risk having your head flushed.

b. Drop out of the cabaret and let Ruby and Becky make idiots of themselves.

c. Do some sort of voodoo spell so that Ruby and Becky come down with a **terrible** but not quite fatal disease.

'I prefer option a,' says Fiona after a little thought. 'That's what a professional would do, I think. But you'll **have** to stick close to me and make sure Becky doesn't get me alone in the girls' toilets.

'Don't worry,' I tell her. 'I will NEVER abandon you.'

There are just a few minutes left before Fiona's mum will arrive so we MUST have a dialogue about our falling out or else it might happen again.

I tell her that I'm sorry if I upset her and explain that I was hurt because I felt betrayed but that I know I should trust her more and be less clingy.

Fiona says that she understands.

'I was a bit insensitive,' she admits, 'Ruby and Becky were horrid to you and I just didn't understand how much they'd hurt you.'

Then we hear the doorbell and we just have time for a big hug before Fiona has to leave.

I am the happiest girl in the UNIVERSE.

14

The next morning at breakfast time there is another knock at the door. This time it's VERY loud.

'I bet I know who that is,' says Dad. 'I'll deal with her.'

Sure enough, it's Mrs Driscoll. I can see her from where I'm peeping through the window. She's in one of her GRIZZLY moods.

'I want you to sign this letter, Mr Codd,' she says, waving a piece of paper at Dad without bothering to say 'good morning', or 'hello' or 'sorry to disturb you', or ANY of the normal, polite things that you might expect.

Dad doesn't take the letter. Instead he puts his hands behind his back.

'Good morning, Mrs Driscoll,' he says. 'What's your letter about?'

Dad knows better than to sign things that Mrs Driscoll brings round. Last time it was a letter to a solicitor. She was trying to get an ASBO against

Joe (that's an anti-social behaviour order and it's BIG trouble if you get one). That was when she said he'd been stealing from her shop, which was ABSOLUTELY not true. I got really angry and tore that letter up, right in front of her, which was pretty bad behaviour but it was a desperate situation. I feel angry again now, just seeing her standing there. I am edging towards the door, ready to pounce if she says anything outrageous.

'I've heard that the school in Wellminster is encouraging wickedness,' she says.

'How would that be, then, Mrs Driscoll?' Dad asks in his 'I-am-trying-to-be-patient voice'.

'They're having a Halloween party,' she says. 'Children will be dressed up as devils and witches and all sorts of terrible things. It has to be stopped!'

I am getting quite close to the door now and I can hear everything that she's saying. It's just like I thought. She is being ridiculous and making trouble. I push in front of Dad saying, 'I'm making the costumes, ACTUALLY, Mrs Driscoll. They're zombies. That's dead people who can't die properly and walk around like this.' I make a face at her and go UUUUGH! 'And there will be vampires and dancing skeletons and wizards and ghosts and every kind of spooky thing you can imagine…and I thought you were moving away soon anyway.'

Dad grabs me by my waist and plonks me behind him saying, 'That's enough, thank you, Coco.'

Mrs Driscoll's eyes have gone narrow and mean. 'I might have known it!' she says. 'I knew you weren't good, decent, respectable people in this house. I should never have come.'

I peek around Dad and say, 'We didn't invite you.'

Dad is trying to push me back in the house and Mum is pulling me from inside whispering, 'Come away, Coco. Calm down. He's not going to sign it.'

'I don't think we can help you, Mrs Driscoll,' Dad says. 'Have a lovely day. Bye now!' He tries to close the door gently, but Mrs Driscoll sticks her arm through so Dad has to open it again to avoid squashing her. She waves another piece of paper at him, saying, 'I'll leave this with you. There's going to be a meeting. I may be leaving Heckaby soon but I must do my best to wipe out evil whilst I'm here.'

Great! Mrs Driscoll thinks she's a superhero.

Just then, GT appears at the top of the stairs in her nightie.

'I heard voices, Deirdre. What's going on?' she says loudly.

Mum is still pulling me into the kitchen as she calls, 'Don't worry, Mum. It's just a neighbour.'

'That's not a neighbour,' GT shouts when she sees Mrs Driscoll. 'That's Hetty Bampton. She's in my class at school. I don't like her. She's a right bossyboots. She stole my dolly mixtures and ate them all. Go away, Bossy Bampton! Clear off, Horrid Hetty!'

Mrs Driscoll stares up at GT, who is now staggering down towards her, hanging onto the bannister. Dad is helping Mum to wrestle me back into the kitchen so that I can't tear up Mrs Driscoll's leaflet or be rude to her again. This means that GT has a clear view of the doorway. She grabs an umbrella that's leaning against the wall and points it at Mrs Driscoll, who looks HORRIFIED.

'You're all mad in this house. Mad and wicked,' she shouts.

'Clear off, Hetty Spaghetti!' says GT. 'You're not having any more of my dolly mixtures!' And she chases Mrs Driscoll up the road in her bare feet and nightie.

Mum lets go of me and panics.

'Stop her, John!' she orders Dad. 'She'll catch a terrible cold.'

'Don't run too quickly, Dad.' I say. 'Let her whack Mrs Driscoll with the brolly first.'

'Coco!' Mum shouts. 'Sit down in that kitchen right now and keep quiet!'

Dad comes back a few minutes later, leading GT gently by the arm. Mum takes her upstairs to wash her feet and put her back to bed for a little while. Dad tells me off for being 'rude and childish' with Mrs Driscoll. He knows I will NEVER apologise to her. He tried to make me do that last time and it was hopeless. He had to give in eventually.

'I know she's a grumpy old thing,' he says, 'but you were being just as horrid as she was, and that makes you look like a brat, doesn't it?'

I wriggle in my chair and sigh. 'I know, but she's such an EXTREME control freak. She can't tell everyone how to behave.'

Dad has to admit that this is true. 'But she'll be moving away in another week or two, so please don't let yourself down by getting angry, Coco.'

'OK,' I agree, but not very happily. 'I'll try.'

Then I give him a smile and ask, 'Did GT manage to hit her with the brolly?'

Dad raises his eyebrows and says, 'No! Thank

goodness. She would probably have had your granny arrested if she had.'

Mrs Driscoll has left her leaflet shoved into our letterbox. I go and fetch it and my blood starts to boil all over again.

'She really IS having a meeting,' I say to Dad, handing him the paper. 'It's at school tomorrow evening. That's our dress rehearsal day! I need to get on that bus quickly and make sure Mr Gampy knows. Witchy Driscoll is going to try and stop the Halloween Cabaret. This is SERIOUS.'

Dad nods. 'She *is* being a party-pooper,' he agrees.

'It's worse than that!' I tell him. 'She's trying to take away our right to celebrate things and have fun!'

Dad nods again, 'So…what are you going to do about it?'

'I'm going to protest.'

'Peacefully?' asks Dad raising his eyebrows sharply, like he is warning me. 'Nothing illegal or violent. I do *not* want to have to fetch you from a police station.'

'Completely peaceful,' I promise him.

Dad claps his hands. 'Good. Peaceful protests are good.'

Then he glances towards the stairs, leans forward and whispers, 'But don't tell Mum. She's got enough to worry about at the moment.'

We shake hands.

I can't wait to get to school and start organising things. On the bus I tell Joe all about Witchy Driscoll's meeting and I ask if he will use his tools to build some placards.

'It won't be a proper protest without wooden placards with slogans on them,' I tell him. 'I'll ask my dad to collect some old wood from the skip and we've got loads of left over paint and nails.'

Joe smiles his lovely film-star smile and agrees. 'No problem. I'll come straight over after dinner. I haven't got any homework tonight.'

Then I text Dad:

Plse cllct wd frm skp fr plcrds. Joe wll
mk thm tnght.
C xxx

Everyone involved in the cabaret has to go to the Drama studio at morning break. Mr Gampy has already heard about the meeting and tells us that quite a lot of people will be going to it, so we have to put the Halloween Cabaret on hold until we know what is decided tomorrow. If the school governors say that it isn't appropriate for our school to celebrate Halloween then it will be cancelled. We are all massively disappointed and FURIOUS.

As soon as the meeting is over I grab Lennox and Gregor, two year-eleven boys who I met in the summer. They're older than me and really popular so if they say we are going to protest, lots of kids will join in. I tell them my plan and they really like it. We start texting everyone we can think of who has anything to do with the cabaret.

> **KEEP THE CABARET!!** prtst mtng Tmrw 4pm B's Bkry nr Bs Stn. Brng yr costms!

Then I text Dad again:

> Prtst defo **ON**. Wll snd frthr instrctns sn. Cx

It's the end of breaktime so we all have to go. Lennox, Gregor and I agree to keep each other up to date and Fiona and I have to dash because it's our time in the lovely Head Space.

'It's a sock-warmer day today,' Fiona says to me. 'Miss Wallcott promised.'

Fortunately Miss Wallcott is a DELICIOUSLY lovely teacher and doesn't get cross about things like being a TINY bit late. We wouldn't want to miss her lessons anyway but ESPECIALLY not today. In the middle of the room the old, round wood-burning stove has been lit and a cosy fire is crackling behind the glass door. We are allowed to sit around with our toes on the fireguard while we read our books. That's what a sock-warmer day is!

HEAVEN!

Unfortunately it's slightly spoiled by Becky, who glares at Fiona and me as we settle down next to each other to read. She probably isn't surprised that Fiona and I are friends again but she isn't going to leave Fiona in peace. She walks past and whispers 'flush-head' into Fiona's ear, which is really OBNOXIOUS. This is a good word to describe that sort of behaviour. It means 'extremely unpleasant', which is exactly what Becky is being. I cannot BELIEVE that this is the same Becky that could be chattering away and smiling at my granny in Goldenboughs in a little while.

There's no sign of Ruby. This is normal. She comes to school more than she used to but she still has LOADS of time off.

We read in silence for the next hour, which is useful because it gives me time to plan the protest in my head while pretending to look through a book about Elizabethan dresses.

Fiona and I stay close together all day and try to avoid the toilets, just in case Becky is prowling, looking for a chance to flush my best friend. At lunchtime Fiona and Becky are summoned to the Art room by Mrs Allen for a disciplinary chat about skipping lessons. I wait in the corridor, hoping to catch another glimpse of the mysterious Mr Finnegan so that I can cheer Fiona up with some gossip afterwards but no luck, he's disappeared again.

Becky comes out first and ignores me, stomping past with her nose in the air. She's trying to look like she doesn't care about being in trouble. Mrs Allen is a bit of a softie, anyway, so I bet she hasn't even given them a detention.

Fiona comes out five minutes later looking a bit shaky.

'What's the verdict?' I ask, anxiously.

'She's going to write to our parents,' Fiona tells me. 'Mum'll be furious.'

'Did you tell Mrs Allen that you only skipped school because Becky threatened you?' I ask.

Fiona shakes her head. 'I let Becky push me into it. It's my own stupid fault.'

'She's pretty scary, though. No one would blame you for doing what she said.'

But Fiona just sighs. She is wearing her best brave and heroic expression, which means that she's going to take responsibility and FACE THE MUSIC. I'm SO proud of her.

When I get home Mum is in the barn. She's talking to one of the builders about how to make sure that the roof is rainproof and safe. I can tell that she's getting ready to stop the building work for a while, which makes me feel sad, like she is putting her dreams away in a box. I leave her to get on with things because she doesn't need me looking

MOPEY and MISERABLE when she's doing this very difficult thing. It's a good time to get on the computer for a news update with Dru.

Dru is probably rushing about getting ready for school right now but it looks like she sent a reply last night.

★ **Dru** to Cordelia

Hi

Aunt Zillah's operation went well. She'll be out of hospital in time for my parents' Halloween party. Dread. This means that as well as my mom's fifteen different pumpkin recipes, all her friends will bring their pumpkin gloop, too. I DO NOT like pumpkin. Esther and I are going to hide in my room and eat popcorn.

How are the zombie costumes going?

Glad the Peter Project went well. Photo?

Love

Dru

xx

PS The puppy is now called Curly!

★ **Cordelia** to Dru

Curly suits him pretty well.

I have **MOMENTOUS** news about Fiona.

I tell her all about how we made friends. Then
I tell her how GT very nearly whacked Witchy
Driscoll with a brolly because she mistook her
for a horrid girl she knew at school and about the
outrageous plan of Witchy Driscoll to try and stop
the cabaret, and OF COURSE I let her know about
the protest. But I have to disappoint her on the
photo of Peter. Never mind.

When this is done I sit in our little kitchen for a
while, waiting for Joe to arrive and quickly getting
my Science homework done while Mr Belly
snore-purrs on my lap, keeping me warm. I can
hear Dad crashing pans around in the restaurant
kitchen. I wonder if we'll have a nice experiment
for dinner. I can smell curry spices and rice
cooking. Yum!

Eventually, Mum comes in from the barn. I'm
just finishing my homework, so her timing is good.
My old baby monitor is clipped to the belt of her
jeans and I must look puzzled when I notice it
because she explains, tapping the pink plastic case,

'I'm using it to keep a check on Granny. I can hear when she wakes up from her naps.'

'Has she been strange today?' I ask.

Mum nods. 'A nurse came round to give me some advice. Granny thought she was a train driver and got upset because she didn't have a ticket. She was worried about being told to get off at the next station. We calmed her down eventually, but it was hard work.'

Joe soon turns up with his tool kit and gets to work in one of the little sheds in our yard. Dad has been great and sorted out some brilliant pieces of wood from the builders' skip. It only takes Joe about an hour to have six big placards ready to write slogans on. Dad comes out to check on us.

'Can you hide these from Mum? I ask him. 'So she doesn't worry.'

Dad taps the side of his nose and says, 'I'll put them in the van. I have to go into Wellminster tomorrow so I'll drop them off at Bessie's. That's where your meeting is, right?'

'Doesn't your mum know about it?' asks Joe.

I shake my head and explain.

'We don't want her to have anything else to stress about right now. She's got enough on her plate with Gran to deal with.'

Joe nods, like he understands. He helps Dad load the van and Dad invites him to stay for dinner, but Joe picks up his tool bag and says, 'Thank you, but I've promised to read my baby brothers a bedtime story.'

Joe is the best big brother in the WORLD. Those sticky twins have no idea how lucky they are.

15

On Thursday morning Fiona sends me a text:

Cn u cm 4 dnnr 2nght? F x

I show it to Mum and she says that's fine as long as I'm home before ten o'clock.

'That means getting the 9.30 bus. OK?' she adds, with a look that says, 'Don't give me any extra stress by being late'.

Fiona and I are just pretending that I'm going to her house for dinner because I need an excuse to be at the protest meeting. Dad knows where I'll be so if I get discovered I hope Mum doesn't go bananas at him for being part of this TEENY WEENY lie.

There is a very TENSE atmosphere around school. Mr Gampy has cancelled the lunchtime rehearsal AND the dress rehearsal tonight! How can he give up so easily? He should have kept rehearsing NO MATTER WHAT. It's a good job we kids

have got lots of energy and DETERMINATION –
determination is a good way to describe how I'm
feeling. It means 'firmness of purpose', according
to our big dictionary at home. That's what I've got,
and what the other kids in the cabaret have got,
too. We are FIRMLY determined to fight off the
party-poopers and have our Halloween Cabaret.
Sometimes adults just seem like they can't be
BOTHERED.

Peter catches up with Fiona and me in the
corridor just before Maths.

'Hey, Cordelia,' he shouts, waving at me over the
sea of people trying to get to their next lesson. 'I was
just about to text you.'

He looks excited. I feel slightly embarrassed
talking to him because of the 'I wouldn't mind
kissing you' thing that he said, but I'm trying to
forget about it and be mature.

'My mum is friends with Bessie, from Bessie's
Bakery,' he tells us. 'She told her about our protest
and Bessie says that we can use the big back room,
behind her kitchen, to have our meeting tonight.
She's going to give us biscuits, too.'

This is BRILLIANT news. We get texting again
straight away to remind everyone to bring their

costumes and so that they know we have a special meeting room and, of course, to tell them about the biscuits. People are MUCH more likely to turn up if you give them a free biscuit.

Peter is beginning to be quite normal. Maybe he's happier now that he has a new image. Who knows? But he's definitely changing for the better.

As I think this I just happen to notice that his eyes are the exact same colour as milk chocolate, but then Becky shoves past and leans into Fiona's ear.

'FLUSSHHH,' she says, in a horrid hissy voice.

Fiona jumps. I immediately forget about Peter's chocolate eyes and think about protecting my best friend.

'Ignore her,' I say, and Becky hears me. She stops and GLARES at me, then at Peter.

'Kissy, kissy,' she says, just like Ruby does, with big, lipsticky lips, and walks away laughing. Fiona must've been thinking the same thing as me because she says, 'She's just copying Ruby, isn't she?'

I nod. 'She's just a copy-cat bully. That makes her a double loser.'

And this time I'm NOT going to get embarrassed about the *kissy kissy* thing. On the outside I stay

calm but inside my head I am imagining myself
SMUDGING Becky's sticky lipstick ALL OVER
her cheeky face WITH AN OLD SOCK!

♥

By afternoon break EVERYONE knows about the
meeting at Bessie's Bakery. Unfortunately, the news
has got through to Becky and Ruby, too. Becky
stops Fiona on the way to French.

'I haven't forgotten about you, flush-head girl,'
she says. 'If you turn up at that protest meeting in a
black dress, you *know* what'll happen. So make sure
you do what I told you, *or else.*'

She marches off and Fiona's bottom lip starts
wobbling. She looks pale and very scared.

'I'll have to carry on with the plan to wear
black, like we decided,' she says 'because I haven't
anything else to wear now. Oh dear!'

'Don't worry,' I tell her. 'NO ONE is going to
flush MY best friend's head and, anyway, Becky
probably won't even be at the protest, she's too lazy.'

Just FIVE METRES further down the corridor,
Ruby stops us.

'I'm not going to your stupid protest,' she says. 'If

the cabaret is going ahead, someone can text me.'

'Who do you think is going to text you?' I say, feeling my old ANGRY self bubbling up, just when I'd been doing so well. 'You've fallen out with all your friends.'

Fiona nudges me, because it's dangerous to talk back to Ruby like this. Her eyes have gone narrow and spiteful. She is ten times scarier than Becky when she's like this.

'Perhaps I'll ask your new boyfriend, Peter Perfect,' she says.

'He's NOT my boyfriend,' I tell her, very firmly, stuffing my hands into my blazer pockets so that I don't PUNCH her (which would lead to INSTANT DEATH). 'It IS possible to be just friends with a boy, you know.'

Ruby sucks her teeth, sneering, and says, 'You would say that, wouldn't you, because you can't even get **him** to be your boyfriend.'

I am about to shout, 'I don't WANT a boyfriend,' but Fiona can obviously see that this is a pointless thing to say to a soup-brain like Ruby and pulls on my sleeve.

'Leave it, Cordelia,' she whispers. 'You'll be wasting your breath.'

She's so right, and I need ALL my breath for the protest. There's always lots of shouting at a protest.

♥

Bessie is AMAZING. She is LIVING PROOF that not all grown-ups think young people are a nuisance. She shows us into the big room behind her kitchen.

'Your dad brought the placards over,' says Bessie. 'And some paint. Be sure you put these cloths on the table and floors before you start…I'll leave you to it.'

People start to arrive and Bessie brings us juice and biscuits AND packets of crisps. Aled turns up with Jamie, and Jamila comes running in, very excited, with Juliette and Alice. Lennox and Gregor are there and lots of the skeleton dancers, and Jason arrives with his mum, but she doesn't stay because she has some shopping to do.

There is LOADS of chatter and excitement and then Peter whispers to me, 'It's your meeting, Cordelia, you'd better get everyone's attention.'

Oh yes! I have to think very fast. I grab the lid of the biscuit tin and find a wooden spoon in one of the drawers behind me. I bash them together,

making a big **CHANG CHANG CHANG** noise.
Everyone jumps, but it seems to work – I've got
their attention.

'OK, sit down and let's get started,' I yell – I have
to yell because it's CHAOS to start with. 'Thank
you for coming, everybody, and thank you to Bessie
for letting us use her room.'

Everyone cheers and claps.

'I suggest that we start by telling each other what
we know about the meeting at school.'

Alice chips in immediately. 'I was told that
there are going to be *hundreds* of grown-ups at the
meeting.'

'Nah,' says Lennox, shaking his head and pulling
a face. 'I bet there's only about six of them.'

'My mum said she thought they might sack Mr
Gampy,' says Jamie.

'WHAT!' shouts everyone at once.

'But she does exaggerate a bit,' Jamie admits, 'so
they probably won't.'

They all start talking at the same time, sharing
what they've heard. It soon gets a bit too noisy so
I **CHANG CHANG** the biscuit lid again with the
wooden spoon because we have to get things done.

'We have to decide what to write on the

placards,' I tell them. 'We've got six.'

Joe lifts one up to show everyone. They all nod and give him a clap to show how impressed they are. Then they all start shouting out their slogan ideas, which makes it IMPOSSIBLE to hear what anyone is saying so I have to **CHANG CHANG** the biscuit tin again and ask them to keep the noise down because there are customers in the café.

We agree to write our ideas on strips of paper and then read them out.

'If an idea gets two votes or more it goes into the biscuit tin,' I explain.

It's a bit like the naming game for Curly the puppy.

'Then we'll shake the tin and pick out the slogans randomly.'

I demonstrate with a slogan that Peter thought up earlier. I write it on a scrap of paper and Fiona reads it out.

'*Halloween is a scream!* Who votes for that?'

Three people put their hands up.

'OK,' I say, 'so that goes in the tin because it got more than one vote.'

Voting takes AGES but eventually we have twelve ideas in the tin and I put the lid on and shake it around. Fiona pulls out six at random and the best painters, supervised by Lennox and Gregor, get to work, painting them onto the placards. They write:

Meanwhile, the rest of us plan what we're going to do when we get to school.

By the time all this is done we only have an hour left before Mrs Driscoll's Anti-Halloween Cabaret Meeting starts in the school hall but none of us are in costume yet. There's a mad scramble while we all unpack our things and get ready. It's one MASSIVE changing room. We are knocking each other with our elbows and tripping over bags and getting our stuff muddled up but SOMEHOW we all get into our costumes and ready to leave. Bessie pops her head round the door.

'Everything OK?' she asks.

Jason is just wiggling into his corset. His lipstick is a bit smudgy and his long, blonde wig isn't quite straight.

'Lovely, thank you, Bessie,' he calls. 'D'you mind if we leave a few things here?'

'As long as they're gone by tomorrow lunchtime,' she agrees, not looking at all worried about the WEIRD sight of us all in our costumes and make-up.

It must be the first time that a crowd like us has got on the bus together in Wellminster. There are two skeletons (Jamie and Aled), a witch (Jamila), a werewolf (Gregor), Frankenstein's monster (Joe), and a couple of vampires (Alice and Lennox), as well as an undertaker in a top hat with a violin (Peter), Jason dressed as a big lady in black satin, and me in one of my zombie tops. I have a plastic axe through my head and I've just had time to stick a few pretend scabs to my face and smear some fake blood on. Fiona looks great in her black dress. Everyone's make-up is a bit of a rushed job but we all look pretty scary – in a funny sort of way.

We get a few strange looks from the other passengers but when Peter starts to play an Irish jig on the violin and walk up and down the bus, they seem to enjoy it. His top hat has a big black ribbon down the back and he's wearing a suit with a tailcoat. I wonder where he got THAT? It's very stylish. Several old ladies start clapping. We can't help giggling. The bus driver must know where we're going because as soon as we get to Wellminster School he shouts.

'Right, you lot. Off!'

And we all jump out.

16

Lennox and Gregor signal to us to duck down behind the wall.

'Go along the side of the kitchen to the back of the sports hall, like we planned,' Lennox reminds us.

We tiptoe all the way, staying low. The changing room door is unlocked so we sneak in and I have to keep saying 'shh' because we've all got the nervous giggles but this is SO important that we mustn't spoil it. When we get inside the changing room I CAN'T BELIEVE what I see. All my zombie waiters have turned up and are in their full costume.

I give a silent HOORAY!

'We thought you were never going to come,' whispers Susan McTay, a big, sensible year-twelve girl. 'We brought some friends.'

We turn round and there are about twenty more big kids hiding in the showers, all in their Halloween costumes, waving and trying not to giggle. There are swamp monsters and more zombies and vampires and werewolves and witches and Ashley Burton, the school football hero, is dressed as Elvis, which isn't very Halloween-ish but never mind. I want to hug them ALL but there isn't time.

'The hall is filling up,' says Fiona, who is sitting on Joe's shoulders so that she can spy through the glass above the door. 'There are about thirty people so far.'

Joe looks a funny shade of purple. He whispers, 'Hurry up! You're heavy.'

Gregor finds a chair for her to stand on instead and Joe looks very relieved but the chair isn't high enough for Fiona to see, so Lennox and I take turns peeking through the glass and listening while Joe and Jason keep people quiet and make sure that everyone knows the plan and what their starting positions should be.

From the chair I can see Mr Okenden sitting at the front, looking a bit nervous and twitchy. Mr Gampy is next to him. He looks tired. Mrs Driscoll has seated herself at the other end of the front row. She's turning round and looking down her nose at people. Then Mr Finnegan walks in calmly, not looking bothered at all. He bends down to whisper something to Mr Okenden, who nods and leans across to pass the message on to Mr Gampy. Mr Finnegan sits down next to Miss Wallcott, which is INTERESTING because they look good together. He is quite handsome, I suppose. But I'll have to save that gossip for another day because Mrs Driscoll is about to speak.

A small group of sour-lemon-faced people applaud softly as she stands up. Peter climbs up on the chair behind me, which is a bit cheeky because it makes it very crowded.

'That guy behind Miss Wallcott is a local counsellor,' Peter tells me. 'That's a bit like an MP but not as important.'

'I know that,' I tell him. 'You're being patronising again.'

'Sorry,' he says. 'And the guy next to him is a newspaper reporter. I've seen him around Wellminster, interviewing people.'

'Now THAT I didn't know,' I admit. 'I hope he's going to report our protest.'

I can only just hear what Mrs Driscoll is saying but I catch 'disgrace' and 'you are inviting the forces of evil into our community'.

GOOD GRIEF! What a lot of nonsense. My dad would be hopping up and down if he heard this. Then I spot him. MY DAD! At the back of the hall! He's not hopping up and down but he's got his extra grumpy face on and his arms are crossed tightly. I bet he's told Mum that he's gone out to buy some eggs or sausages, or something.

A man sitting a few rows behind Mr Okenden stands up and interrupts Mrs Driscoll, shouting, 'I don't care about all that stuff, it's the parking that bothers me. It'll be chaos. I live across the road and I won't be able to get into my drive.'

Then a lady just in front of him springs up and butts in.

'I don't want them trick or treating up our street,' she calls out. 'They'll be knocking on the doors, demanding sweets and frightening the old folks.'

'There'll be vandalism!' someone else shouts.

'My garden gnomes were stolen last year!' shouts another.

Dad just keeps his arms folded and rolls his eyes a lot. He probably thinks they're all talking rubbish.

One by one grumpy grown-ups stand up and shout out their complaints until no one is listening to Mrs Driscoll any more because they're too busy trying to talk over each other. She starts to turn purple, then screws up her notes and walks back to her seat in a huff. Mr Okenden has to calm things down.

'I think, ladies and gentlemen,' he begins, 'that we've heard quite a few of the arguments against having a Halloween cabaret. Perhaps we could now hear the other side. Mr Gampy?'

Mr Gampy gets up to speak but the sour-lemon-people don't clap him. I hear him say something about 'just having a party to raise money for books', but Mrs Driscoll calls out, 'You are a *frivolous fop*, Mr Gampy, and you are leading our children into darkness.'

Peter puts his hand over his mouth to stop himself giggling. I'm not sure what a *frivolous fop* is but I'm not going to ask Peter because he'd be such a know-all about it, so I'll have to get the dictionary later.

The grown-ups start shouting across the hall at each other again and not listening to Mr Gampy or to each other. He does his best to finish his speech but he looks quite relieved when he can sit down again.

Mr Okenden introduces Mr Finnegan who gets up slowly. Perhaps because of the mystery surrounding him, everyone goes quiet. I bet they're all wondering which side he will be on. Using his walking stick he makes his way to the front. I whisper to the protest team, 'Are you ready?'

They all nod.

'Starting positions,' I say. 'Silently. Remember to wait for the violin.'

They all give me a thumbs-up.

Mr Finnegan is speaking. I notice that everyone listens when Mr Finnegan speaks. There is something about him that makes you think he is going to say something useful, so you want to hear it.

'The festival of Halloween,' he begins, and looks around the room at everyone, 'is celebrated to help us not to fear death. When we dress up in frightening costumes and dance around or play games we are saying, "We all know that we will die one day, eventually, but at the moment we are alive and we are enjoying it."'

This is BRILLIANT. Mrs Driscoll is crossing her legs and uncrossing them, looking very fidgety and uncomfortable. Mr Finnegan goes on.

'If we stopped doing things simply because other people don't like them, then no one would ever do anything *new* or *interesting* or *different*, and what a boring world that would be. As long as we do not hurt each other or steal from each other or lie about each other then we should not be prevented from having fun in whatever way we choose.'

Peter and I jump off the chair quietly. He picks up his violin and gets ready to play while I hold the door handle. I signal to him and he starts playing. He plays wild, fast music as he marches through the open door to the hall with his black ribbon and coat tails flowing. He is closely followed by Joe, dressed as Frankenstein's monster, wheeling Jason, who is lying on his side on one of the lunch trollies. We all come in behind them and spread ourselves around the hall.

Jason is waving his right arm, flashing his black nail polish and spangled cocktail rings.

The people in the hall either giggle or gasp with horror, depending on whether they are for or against the cabaret. None of them move for a while, which gives Jason a chance to jump off the trolley and head for the stage. Some of the sour-lemon-people are already pulling their coats on and getting ready to walk out.

Jason climbs onto the stage and prepares to sing. At the same time, a *tap-tap-tapping* starts on the windows on the far side of the hall, then it becomes a *bang-bang-rattling*. Everyone looks that way and sees an army of zombies squashing their faces onto the glass, as if they're trying to get in. Some of them are wearing MY COSTUMES, and they look BRILLIANT. Mr Okenden pretends to ignore them at first, but you can't ignore a zombie invasion, can you? Not when they're groaning and rattling the door handles.

While the audience is distracted by the zombie army, Lennox plugs his player into the wall and puts 'Monster Mash' on really LOUDLY. Peter stops playing the violin and comes to stand with the rest of us. Fiona and the skeleton dancers take their places beside Jason as he starts singing. He is such a FREAKY sight that everyone's eyes are glued to his big, black, slinky dress and massive blonde wig.

The zombies stagger in from the inside corridor, some with their arms stretched out in front and some waving placards. They march round and round the hall so that all the grown-ups have time to read our slogans and then they stagger to the front to join in the dancing.

Gregor the werewolf tries to cuddle Mrs Driscoll

and Lennox the vampire pretends to bite a lady's neck. Neither of them finds this funny and Mrs Driscoll hits Gregor the werewolf over the head with her handbag. He lets out a HOWWWL as she wallops him.

Mr Okenden seems to be going into SHOCK because he hasn't moved and there are kids in Halloween costumes dancing all around him, singing. I think I see Mr Gampy hiding a giggle behind his hand. Mr Finnegan gives a mysterious smile and Miss Wallcott is grinning from ear to ear until she sees Mrs Driscoll start bashing the werewolf with her handbag and rushes over to calm things down.

Some of the parents stand up and join in with the clapping and dancing, but the sour-lemon-people are trying to leave. Several witches and Elvis block the door. The sour-lemons who have escaped are being chased across the car park by Joe, stomping after them in his Frankenstein's monster boots and ROARING. Mrs Driscoll has turned purple and is shouting at Mr Gampy but no one can hear her because of the music. It's CHAOS. It's completely bonkers but Jason and Fiona sound great and the dancers are all in time, and it feels like a

BIG,CRAZY PARTY is starting, until Mrs Driscoll unplugs the music.

Everything suddenly STOPS.

Oooh! That woman is HORRID.

There are a few seconds where nobody says anything and nobody moves. Then Mr Okenden coughs and says, 'Perhaps we could all return to our seats and we'll take a vote.'

He looks at Mr Gampy with a deep frown, as if he is saying, 'I blame you for this'. I can't hear what Mr Gampy says but I watch his lips and I think it's, 'I really had no idea they were planning this.'

I don't think Mr Okenden believes him. Mr Gampy might be in BIG trouble later.

We protesters all gather together at the front and hold our placards up. Peter plays slow, sad music on the violin, very quietly.

The grown-ups sit down again. Some of the sour-lemon-people come back in from the car park. There's a lot of chattering and giggling and some tut-tutting going on but Mr Okenden keeps talking, trying to get control of things. Eventually, everyone calms down and Peter stops playing.

Mr Okenden straightens his dark-blue tie and

says, 'Right…well, I think we can see what the pupils at Wellminster want but let's have a show of hands, shall we? All those who feel that the celebration of Halloween is *inappropriate* at our school, please raise your hands now.'

I count the hands…Eleven. Some of the sour-lemon squad have already left. Hooray! More votes for us. But is it going to be ENOUGH? The zombies shuffle to the end of the rows where the sour-lemon-anti-Halloween-voters are sitting, and point at them, staring and making **ughh ughh** noises while Peter makes squeaky violin sounds close to their ears.

'Stop that!' calls Mr Okenden. 'You've made your point. And may I remind you that pupils do **not** have a vote.'

We all groan. The zombies make **ughh ughh** noises again and the werewolf HOWWWLS, Frankenstein's monster stamps his boots and the witches shakes their broomsticks. One of them shouts, 'BAT WINGS AND FROG BRAINS!'

Mr Okenden gives us his big, deep frown and we all shut up.

'All those who feel that the celebration of Halloween is harmless fun,' says Mr Okenden, 'and

229

that the cabaret evening should continue, please raise your hands.'

Everyone who is still there and ISN'T a sour lemon puts their hand up. There is a two second silence while we all count. I count:

Nine…ten…eleven…twelve…thirteen!

We give a MASSIVE cheer. The zombies shake their placards, Peter squeaks the violin, vampires flap their cloaks, Frankenstein's monster stamps his boots again, a witch shouts, 'HA HA HA! WE WIN!' Jason wiggles his hips and makes a **whoop whoop** sound and I jump up and down trying to hug everyone at once.

Mr Okenden gives his big, deep frown again and we stop. The scraping sound of chairs being pushed back fills the hall as the UTTERLY DEFEATED sour-lemon-people storm out in a huff. They're probably going to have a good old moan and write a stroppy letter to the local paper or something, but NOBODY CARES.

'Very well,' says Mr Okenden, over the noise of scraping chairs and muttering voices. 'It seems that the Halloween Cabaret will go ahead for this year.'

Mr Gampy has found a microphone.

'Thank you very much for coming, everyone. We now need to start getting the hall ready and to prepare for our dress rehearsal with **considerable urgency**, and we'll have to work very fast to get the hall decorated. Could everyone involved in the cabaret please get ready to rehearse and if there are any parents who have time to help with the decorations, your assistance would be very welcome.'

After we have finished jumping up and down and cheering we start texting around to spread the word that the cabaret is definitely going ahead and anyone who isn't here needs to get to school fast for the dress rehearsal.

One of the school secretaries, Mrs Choudhray, puts the word out on the school Facebook and Twitter accounts and starts telephoning everyone she can think of to prepare snacks and drinks for tomorrow.

'Don't worry,' she says. 'We'll have more samosas and crisps than we can possibly eat, and enough juice to fill a swimming pool.'

I nearly forget to talk to Dad so I rush over and give him a hug.

'Thanks for coming,' I say. 'Where does Mum think you are?'

'She knows I'm here,' he says.

'Oh no! How did she find out?' I ask.

'She saw you getting on the bus when she was driving back home. She'd been posting leaflets for the restaurant through doors in Wellminster. It gave her a break from looking after Gran.'

I bite my bottom lip. 'Was she VERY upset and stressy?'

He shakes his head. 'No, she was just very cross with me for not telling her and said I should get down here and support you, straightaway.'

That's a relief! My mum isn't as much of a stress-head as I expect her to be sometimes.

'I brought you some sandwiches,' he says, handing me a massive lunchbox.

I open it straight away because I'm STARVING.

'Thank you!' I mumble through a mouthful of lovely tomato and chicken – my dad makes the BEST sandwiches in the world.

'I like that Mr Finnegan,' Dad tells me, as he

unwraps a carton of apple juice for me and sticks the straw in.

'Oh yes, he's BRILLIANT, isn't he?' I say.

I tell Dad about the mystery that surrounds Mr Finnegan.

'He had some kind of dangerous adventure involving pirates,' I tell him. 'That's why he has a scar and a limp.'

Dad gives me his 'I don't believe you' look and sniffs.

'He probably just had too much beer and fell out of a taxi.'

'Dad, don't spoil it!' I say. 'You're just jealous because Mum will fancy him.'

His face changes. He is frowning. Perhaps I shouldn't have said this, even though it was a joke. I forgot, for a millisecond, that Dad is trying VERY hard to make Mum fall in love with him again.

'Will she?' he asks, going a tiny bit pink – so I can tell that he's trying not to be jealous.

'ALL the mums will fancy Mr Finnegan. Don't worry,' I say, quickly, to make things better. 'And I'm sure Mum fancies you MUCH more.'

'Perhaps I'll ask her out on a date, then,' Dad

says, with his jokey smile back again. 'I've heard there's a good Halloween party going on here tomorrow.'

'Yes! Brilliant idea,' I tell him. 'Go home now and ask her. Thanks for the sandwich. Go!' and I give him a little push, which makes him laugh.

17

We're all buzzing with excitement at the start of the dress rehearsal. Becky and Ruby arrive at the last minute, after all the hard work of the protest has been done by other people. *QUELLE SURPRISE!* (That's a way of being sarcastic in French and it means 'what a surprise!' when you're not really surprised at all.) They don't look at each other and they keep their coats on.

Becky is wearing MASSIVE false eyelashes that are green, like a peacock's bottom and Ruby is struggling to keep her balance on the most gigantically high shoes I have EVER seen. Fiona is standing next to me, behind Joe and Gregor and Lennox, just in case there is trouble when the MEAN GIRLS spot that she is wearing her lovely LBD (Little Black Dress).

Jason has his wig and lipstick on properly now. But... *QUELLE HORREUR!* (you can probably guess what that means), Jason suddenly pulls a face like he has just seen a car accident. Fiona's eyebrows are nearly on the ceiling. Everyone, including Mr Gampy, stares as Ruby and Becky take off their coats.

Becky is wearing a long, Barbie-pink and canary-yellow dress covered in sequins that are so bright and twinkly that Ashley Burton, the boy dressed as Elvis, puts his sunglasses on and Peter pulls his top hat down over his face. She looks like a firework!

Ruby towers above her, balancing on her shoes. She has swapped the green Christmas tree dress for a silver-and-gold sparkly mini-mini-mini dress and I can't help looking at her legs – they're ORANGE – she's obviously been experimenting with fake tan. Oh dear!

Becky and Ruby look like Cinderella's ugly sisters dipped in glitter – a fashion DISASTER. Mr Gampy is FURIOUS.

'I **specifically** told you to wear black,' he tells them.

Ruby and Becky point at each other and say, 'She's not!'

Fiona is looking worried.

'I can't hide here all night,' she whispers to me.

I squeeze her hand to reassure her and she sneaks

up onto the stage and stands near Jason, ready to sing. Becky and Ruby don't notice her because they're still arguing with Mr Gampy.

'Black's boring, sir,' says Ruby with a sneer.

'That's the point,' he says. His voice sounds more and more fed up. 'You are **backing** singers,' he says. 'You go at the **back**, **behind** the main singer. You **blend** into the **background** so that everyone is looking at Jason, not **you**. Go and get changed immediately.'

'But sir,' Becky starts.

Mr Gampy lifts his hand and turns his face away. 'I don't want to hear whatever your pathetic excuses are. Just get changed or go home, now.'

'I spent a lot of money on this, sir!' Becky says, VERY loudly.

More like WASTED a lot of money, I think to myself.

'That's **your** problem, not mine,' says Mr Gampy. 'You should have followed my instructions.'

Becky turns to Ruby and yells, 'This is your fault!'

Ruby's mouth drops open, as if she has NO IDEA what Becky is talking about.

'I didn't tell you what to wear,' Ruby shouts back.

'You told me not to wear black. You said if I did, you'd flush the toilet on my head.'

She turns to Mr Gampy. 'She did, sir.'

Fiona is now the one looking shocked. She steps forward. I wish she wouldn't. Oh no! What will the poisonous pair do when they see her? I freeze, and get ready to rush in and save her from them.

'Becky Freemantle!' Fiona shouts. 'You are a second-hand bully. You said you'd flush *my* head! But you clearly only said it because Ruby said she would flush *yours*. You can't even think up your own, original nasty stuff – you have to nick ideas from Ruby!'

Mr Gampy waves his arms to signal STOP!

'**No one** is flushing **anyone's** head. Got that?' he says.

But Fiona has started now. It's as if her lid has popped off and she's fizzing with anger at Becky. 'You should have stood up to Ruby, like I stood up to you,' Fiona tells her. 'Then we'd both be wearing black and Ruby would be the one looking a **twit**. Instead, you let her push you around and now you look a **prize noddy**, just like her. It's your own fault, Becky.'

That was quite an impressive speech. I'm feeling really proud of my best friend.

But Mr Gampy has had ENOUGH.

'Fiona, keep out of this, please. Ruby and Becky, go home. You are both out of the cabaret. Off you go!'

Fiona does as he says but Ruby and Becky don't move at first, they just stare at each other like they are about to have a fight.

'Go on. The pair of you,' says Mr Gampy. 'Now!'

They storm off towards the changing rooms. Ruby clomps along in her HUGE shoes and Becky's false eyelashes start sticking together with her angry tears. She can't see where she's going and bumps into the lunch trolley that Jason was wheeled in on, then she swears VERY badly, and limps out. We hear them yelling at each other on the other side of the door.

So now Fiona is the only backing singer.

Mr Gampy sighs DEEPLY. He looks like he needs to sleep for about two weeks. He asks, 'Can you manage on your own, Fiona?'

My AMAZING best friend takes a deep breath.

'Yes,' she says, 'no problem.'

Mr Gampy is about to thank her when a very loud **FLUSSSHHH!** sound comes from the direction of the changing rooms, followed by another, and ANOTHER and then a SCREAAAM! Becky runs out and across the hall, sopping wet and dripping water EVERYWHERE. Ruby is chasing her – she's taken off her huge shoes so that she can run – she's dripping wet, too, and they're both sobbing and yelling REALLY BAD SWEAR WORDS. They must have FLUSHED each other. Mr Finnegan and Miss Wallcott stop them at the door and march them off somewhere. Who knows where? Who CARES? The rest of us have a show to put on.

I'm so excited after the dress rehearsal that I'm WIDE AWAKE until WAY past bedtime so I sneak downstairs when Mum is asleep and write to Dru to update her on the success of our protest. First, I read her latest news.

★ **Dru** to Cordelia

It's **EXTRAFANTABULOUS** that you

and Fiona are friends again - Hooray!
It made me happy all day!

I've attached a photo of Esther and
me carving a pumpkin-head lantern.
D'you like it? This is the only good
use for a pumpkin. I still can't
believe that people eat it!

The other photo is one that my
teacher helped me to take at Astronomy
Club. Esther and I have just joined.
Space is **MIND-BOGGLING**, isn't it? I
love looking at it.

Hug you!!

Dru

Xx

The pumpkin is ENORMOUS and it has lots of
teeth. It looks CREEPY with the light inside, and
Dru's space photo is INCREDIBLE. It's a whole
galaxy whirling in a coloured spiral. I write back and
tell her how fantastic I think these are and then fill
her in on the news about our protest and the dress
rehearsal and ESPECIALLY about the DOUBLE
FLUSHING incident, which makes me giggle to
myself. Then I finish by asking:

How's Curly the puppy doing? Is your Aunt Zillah
with you now? Do they like each other?

Happy Halloween!

C

xx

I still wake up REALLY early. I'll just have to get
through the Halloween Cabaret on batteries of
EXCITEMENT because I've only had a few hours
sleep. At least Hitler didn't wake us up last night.

GT is already in the kitchen when I get
downstairs. She's mashing Weetabix and grapefruit
juice together in a bowl using a fork and making a
big mess.

'Morning, Deirdre,' she calls, pouring more juice
out of the carton into the bowl. 'You forgot to feed
Timmy again.'

Mr Belly is looking up at her from under the
table, licking his lips. Perhaps GT once had a cat
called Timmy. I don't know, but Mr Belly is going
to get a NASTY surprise when he sees what's
for breakfast. Our cat is DEFINITELY not a
vegetarian.

242

'I think he prefers this,' I tell her, hurrying to the cupboard and pulling out a tin of turkey-giblet-and-rabbit-flavoured cat food.

GT takes a quick look at the tin and frowns, saying, 'Oh, I don't think so.'

She looks at Mr Belly and smiles. 'You always have the same cereal as me, don't you, Timmy?'

I want to shout, 'HIS NAME IS NOT TIMMY,' but there doesn't seem much point. It will just make GT all upset and confused. Mr Belly purrs and gets ready to jump up. He is going to be SO disappointed when he finds that SMUSH in his bowl. His day is NOT going to start well.

I put some bread in the toaster and watch as he sniffs his bowl when GT puts it down for him. He looks up at me and meows in a way that I am CERTAIN is a swear word in cat language. I'm not surprised.

Mum has gone out early to visit Goldenboughs again so Dad will be watching GT this morning. He comes down from the shower just as my toast pops up and starts making his usual SUPER STRONG breakfast coffee.

'Morning, Coco,' he says, and kisses the top of my head. Then he notices what a mess GT has

made and starts cleaning up. He scrapes splashes
of cereal smush off the worktop and the cupboard
doors. There are splots on the table and the floor as
well. He gives me a puzzled look and points to the
cloth he is wiping with.

'Gran was feeding Mr Belly,' I explain in a
whisper. 'But I don't think he was impressed.'

GT is by the window now, on Planet Typewriter,
so I tip the gooey contents of Mr Belly's bowl into the
bin and fill it with the turkey giblet and rabbit food.

He rushes over and tucks in. I'm sure he would
say, 'Phew! Thank you!' if he could.

I call, 'Bye, Granny,' but GT doesn't seem to hear
me. I nearly go without trying again but something
makes me change my mind. I step over to her and
wait for her to stop typing for a second before
putting my hand on her shoulder. She spins around
and looks at me, a little bit surprised. I see right into
her pale-blue eyes.

'Bye, Granny,' I say again and give her a kiss on
the forehead.

She looks a bit faraway and puzzled, but she
smiles and says, 'What a lovely young lady. What's
your name?'

'Cordelia.'

'Goodbye, Cordelia, my dear,' she says, and goes back to her typing.

♥

When I meet up with Fiona by the car park she blurts out, 'My mum got the letter Mrs Allen sent yesterday!'

I gasp. 'How did she take it?'

Fiona shakes her head, 'Badly. She nearly stopped me doing the cabaret.'

'What? Wow! She must've been REALLY angry to do that. What did she say?'

'A lot,' says Fiona, rolling her eyes. 'I got a complete ear-bending and if I ever do it again I'll be grounded **forever**. Seriously, no more going to Bessie's for cake, no more sleepovers, nothing. I'm going to have to be a complete angel for months and months.'

'Well, you ARE a complete angel most of the time,' I tell her, 'so I don't think you need to worry.'

She sighs. 'Thanks.'

And we make our way to registration quickly because we don't want her getting in trouble for being late.

After registration we head off for Science quickly but we bump straight into Becky and Ruby walking out of the girls' toilets TOGETHER. They've missed registration but that's their problem. *Our* problem is that it looks like they're friends again. How did that happen? This means double trouble.

They block our way and stare at Fiona. Nobody moves. Then Becky holds up a little black dress.

'That's my dress!' Fiona yells. 'I left it in the changing rooms last night!'

Becky lifts it up and RIPS it right down the back. The zip gets mangled and the seam is hopelessly torn.

I cannot believe she did that. Fiona's mouth drops open with shock. Becky hands her the dress and she and Ruby just turn and walk away.

My face is going beetroot-pink. I am counting in my head to stop myself from strangling them – one…two…three…I am REALLY struggling to hold my temper in. It's going to blow. I can't help it. HERE IT COMES. At first it squeezes out in a VERY firm voice from between my clenched teeth. I growl after them, 'How does it feel to be kicked off the cabaret, losers?'

They stop, turn back and walk towards me. I may

be about to DIE. Ruby looks at her long nails, then at me.

'We couldn't care less,' she says. 'The whole thing is going to be a **pile of poo**, anyway. We're not even coming to watch.'

'Good. It'll be great NOT seeing you there,' I snap back. I am really living dangerously.

Ruby pulls a sneery face at both of us.

'Leave it, Cordelia,' says Fiona, 'I have another dress I can wear.'

But I know that she LOVED that dress, so I'm pretty sure she's just being brave and trying to avoid a big scene.

Ruby pulls a leaflet out of her pocket. It's the advertisement for the Jug and Monkey, the leaflet my mum and dad wrote and printed and spent hours and hours posting through letterboxes. She holds it in front of my face and slowly tears it into little, tiny pieces, dropping the ragged bits on the floor. They immediately get kicked and trampled and carried off on people's shoes.

She has just TORN UP my parents' hard work.

I can feel Fiona's hand on my arm, gently holding me back from PULLING RUBY'S EARS OFF with my bare hands.

'I'm going to give your dad's restaurant a STINKING review on the internet,' Ruby says, 'the whole world will know that **dog food** taste better than his cooking!'

And she flicks her chin up, saying, 'C'mon, Becky, this is boring.'

Becky follows her as they strut off down the corridor.

'No one would believe anything YOU wrote!' I yell after her. 'Everyone knows you're a first class, gold-plated FIBBER.'

But they ignore me.

'How do some people even think up such nastiness?' I ask Fiona. 'Their brains must be made of PICKLED CAT SICK.'

Fiona just shakes her head and stares down at her hands, where the remains of her cabaret dress flop like a dishrag. I watch the last bits of leaflet get scuffed and dragged away.

The day goes SLOWLY. Fiona and I avoid the toilets just in case we're ambushed by Ruby and Becky. We meet up with Peter and Joe near the car park at breaktimes. Fiona admits that she hasn't really got another dress to wear but I remind her that I've got one that should fit her and I'll ask my parents to bring it tonight. I REALLY hope it does fit, I want her to look FABBY–DOO on stage.

We all agree that it's a DISASTER that Ruby and Becky are friends again, but we all know it won't last and we promise ourselves that there is NO WAY they will spoil the cabaret for any of us. It's SO much easier to keep strong when you have friends on your side.

The final bell rings AT LAST. I forget about Ruby and Becky for a while because my heart is skipping with excitement. I called Mum at lunchtime to ask if she or Dad could POSSIBLY bring my black dress for Fiona and Dad drives over especially to deliver it as soon as school finishes, then gets ready to whizz back home, saying, 'I have to get into my costume, too, y'know?'

'What is it?' I call through the car window.

'A surprise!' he says, laughing, and drives off.

But I don't have time to worry about it because I have to dash back to the hall to help with the finishing touches to the decorations. Before I know it, it's nearly time, and we're all crammed into the changing rooms getting ready.

The dress fits Fiona PERFECTLY. It's longer on

her than on me, and it looks very sophisticated that way – *'trés chic'*.

Mum and Dad arrive early to help set out the tables. As soon as I see them I give a little squeal and run over because Mum looks BEAUTIFUL. No wonder Dad wants her to fall in love with him again.

'Where did you get that dress?' I ask, with big, greedy eyes.

'I thought you'd like it,' she says, smiling. 'I've had it for years and years. It's been lying in a suitcase wrapped up in tissue paper.'

Mum's costume is a long, red velvet dress that fits very tightly. Her hair is straight and a bit Goth-looking and she has put pale face powder on. There's a transfer on her neck of two bite marks and a trickle of blood. Dad can't stop looking at her dress, which is a good sign. Perhaps this is the night that Mum will let him get romantic again. But when Dad takes off his coat and I see HIS costume, I'm not so sure that Mum will want to go near him. It makes me jump out of my skin.

He's wearing his old chef's whites – trousers and a jacket that buttons up to the neck. They are COVERED in fake blood and he's carrying a pretend meat cleaver (that's like an axe for chopping through bones). He looks PSYCHO-TERRIFYING! If he wasn't my dad I'd RUN.

'I wish Granny could have come, too.' I say, feeling a bit sad for her. I'm surprised at how differently I feel about her now. Talking to her just a little bit has made me see that she needs to be loved, just like everyone else. So, if she knows we care about her then she'll be happier, won't she? And if she's happy she won't get grumpy and snap at us. I think Dru would be quite proud of me for thinking like this.

Dad squeezes my shoulder, gently. 'I think she'd find it very confusing and tiring,' he says, 'and she's happy watching Laurel and Hardy for a little while.'

'I'm just staying for an hour, Coco,' says Mum. 'I'd like to stay to the end but I can't leave Granny too long.'

I tell Mum it's fine because even though I really want her to stay I'm grown-up enough to see that she has go. There's no point being cross about it.

Mum has brought me some make-up to borrow, including her dark plum-coloured lipstick. I have to dash into the changing rooms now and put it on because I haven't got much time. I use LOADS of it.

It's not exactly pretty but it's very Halloweeny and goes well with my zombie T-shirt and torn leggings.

She's also made me a necklace with the big rubber spider from the joke shop. It's dangling on a long, black bootlace. I love it!

There's just time for me to double check that all my zombies have got their hair and make-up right, and to help Gregor the Werewolf and Joe the Monster to put their masks on before we all have to be in position for the start of the show. I climb onto a chair and peek through the glass above the changing room door.

All the tables are covered with black paper cloths and the Halloween bunting we made in Mrs Allen's class is up. Little pumpkin lights sit at the centre of each table and someone has made the basketball hoop into a gallows. A plastic skeleton is hanging from it by his neck, dressed in rags. It's GENIUS. We have spooky green lava lamp projections on the ceiling that make changing, blobby, swampy patterns, and Michaela, who's in year eleven, has set up another projector that is showing a black and white film called *Son of Frankenstein* without the sound, just the pictures playing as people come in and take their seats.

Mr Gampy knocks on the changing room door.

'Are the zombie waiters ready?' he asks. 'Time to start serving drinks, please.'

They stagger out looking really YUCK, which is perfect. I think I've done a pretty good job.

The hall starts to fill up with parents and kids in fancy dress, all giggling and excited. Peter walks around playing his violin while the werewolf and the witches and Frankenstein's monster follow people about and make them jump. The atmosphere gets even better when the lights go down and before I know it, Mr Gampy is up on stage, dressed in a big black cloak and carrying a huge scythe.

'Ladies and gentlemen, spectres, phantoms, ghouls, goblins, witches and other creatures of the night…Welcome to our Halloween Cabaret!'

And the best party night of my LIFE begins.

There are skeleton dancers and a juggling vampire, singing werewolves and acrobats dressed as black cats. There's a scary poem competition and some year-twelve girls do the three witches scene from

Shakespeare's *Macbeth* with lots of dry ice and green smoke.

Mum has to leave just after this so she misses the pumpkin bingo, where Mrs Allen, dressed as a fortune-teller pulls the numbers out of a giant pumpkin head. Dad wins a pumpkin pie! I don't think Dru would be very impressed but it looks tasty to me.

Mum also misses Fiona and Jason doing the big finale. I'm nervous for Fiona when she takes her place on the stage. She looks calm on the outside. Perhaps I'm feeling her butterflies for her. It's wonderful when her voice harmonises with Jason's. The audience clap because they sound so AMAZING together. When they reach the chorus of 'Monster Mash' all the rest of the performers and the zombie waiters join in the dancing, and then the audience get up and start dancing too, and it all ends with everyone laughing and dancing. Some of the kids look a bit embarrassed when their parents join in, which I completely understand, but by the time everyone is leaving it's obvious that, despite the embarrassing parents, the whole evening was a total SUCCESS.

18

It isn't very late when we get home. The whole show is over in a couple of hours and the school caretaker soon shouts through the changing room doors, 'I need you all out in fifteen minutes or you'll be locked in for the night.'

Joe's parents drop me and Dad off at home. We say thank you then stand for a moment under the clear night and the bright stars, waving to the back of their car and listening to the sound of its engine fading.

'You run ahead and start getting ready for bed, Coco,' Dad says when we can't hear the engine any more. 'I'll just check that everything is secure in the barn.'

I gently push the front door open and tiptoe into our tiny living room so I don't make too much noise. I can hear the buzz of the television but no sounds of people talking or music, just that fuzzy humming you get when a DVD has ended or is paused. GT is asleep in the armchair. Mum is sitting, holding her hand, looking at it and stroking it gently. I'm feeling really happy because everything went PERFECTLY tonight and I'm not tired at all, so I think, perhaps, it would be nice to help Mum to get GT to bed, or to have a chat with her, if she recognises me.

On the screen, Stan Laurel is frozen, lifting his hat and scratching his head. GT's eyes are closed and her mouth is open a little bit. She looks peaceful so I stand near the door for a moment where I won't disturb her sleep. Mum hasn't noticed I'm here yet because I'm being so quiet. I'm listening to hear if GT is snoring. Her eyes will open any second and her face will change when she sees me. Mum will spot me first. I wait a bit longer, just a few seconds, then I step closer. Nothing happens. Mum still hasn't noticed me. GT must be very deeply asleep. I watch her but she doesn't move at all, not even a tiny part of her is moving. I take another step towards her and wait again, and that's when I realise that she's not asleep. She isn't breathing. That's when I know that she's dead.

I've never seen a dead person before and my brain isn't sure of what my eyes are seeing but somewhere, deep down inside me, much deeper down than my brain or my eyes I just know that Granny Twigg isn't inside her body any more. Don't ask me where she's gone, that's a whole MASSIVE question, but all that is in the chair is Granny's body with no breathing in her chest and no thoughts in her head and no pumping in her heart. Sometimes you can be certain of something without any proof, just a very strong feeling inside.

I take two steps forward then and Mum hears and turns to me. Her eyes are shiny with tears. She reaches out to hold my hand, squeezes it and whispers, 'Granny's gone, Coco.'

Dad comes in just then. When he sees us he must be able to tell what's happened straight away because he holds me very close, saying, 'It's OK, Coco. It's OK.'

Mum looks up at Dad and nods.

'When did she go?' he asks quietly

'Just ten minutes ago,' says Mum. 'She was sleeping but she opened her eyes and smiled, then closed them again. I put the kettle on for her hot water bottle and when I turned to ask her if she wanted some cocoa, she'd gone.'

Mum reaches into her bag, pulls out her phone and hands it to Dad.

We have a group cuddle, silently, while a phone rings faintly in the distance down the mobile. I don't feel like crying, not just now. This isn't sinking in yet. How long does that take, I wonder? How should I be feeling? I've never been through this before. It's not the sort of thing that you can practise, is it? But I can't help thinking, as I'm cuddled up against Mum and Dad, that, with Mum still in her red velvet dress, Dad in his psycho chef outfit and me in my dark lipstick and zombie top, we look like we've been sent by Mr Death to collect Granny but she left while we were still at the party.

It's when I come down the next morning for breakfast and there's no typing, no eggy smell, and no muddled conversation about car factories or sandwiches or Hitler or Hetty Spaghetti the school bully, that I realise that GT has really gone and all those things have gone with her, forever.

Dad slept on the floor of our tiny living room last night, in a sleeping bag, so that I wouldn't be alone. Mum had to go in the ambulance to the hospital, where they'll keep GT's body until it is taken away to get it ready for her funeral.

I can hear the plumbing clonking and bubbling so Mum must be in the shower. I think she's been out all night because she wasn't in bed when I woke up and her nightie was still on her pillow, neatly folded up. Dad is making her some breakfast. We're both moving slowly and speaking quietly.

'Where d'you think Gran is now?' I ask Dad as I sip some juice and nibble a piece of dry toast. Neither of us is very hungry.

'That's a big question, Coco,' he says, as he warms the teapot. 'No one really knows where we go when we die.'

'But where do you THINK she is?' I ask.

'Well,' he stares into the teapot as he swirls the water around, 'I believe that when we die we go back into the universe, like drops of water being poured into an ocean.'

I think about the whirling galaxy in the photo Dru sent. I like Dad's idea. It doesn't sound lonely, just peaceful, turning around gently with the stars.

Mum is pale and quiet when she joins us in the kitchen. I give her a long cuddle and don't ask for anything. After breakfast she has a nap and we stay quiet so that we don't disturb her, then Dad helps her to pack all GT's belongings away.

While they do this I send Dru my news. I want to write it down before I tell anyone, even Fiona because it helps me to feel calmer when I write things down first.

★ **Cordelia** to Dru

Hope you had a great Halloween. I will never forget this one...

And I tell her that GT has died, and how I feel like my insides are a jacket potato that has been scooped out and I'm just like the skin, left empty and gone cold.

And Mum and Dad are being ever so quiet and moving very slowly because we're all in terrible shock, I suppose.

Love

C x

Dru writes back to me straight away. She must be up in the middle of the NIGHT – sometimes her enormous brain won't stop working and it keeps her awake. It must be about one-thirty in the morning over there! I bet her parents don't know that she's on the computer.

★ **Dru** to Cordelia

Oh, Cordelia, I'm **SO SORRY** about
your Granny!

It sounds like she was very happy
when she died, watching Laurel and
Hardy and sitting in a comfy chair.
And she had you guys taking care of
her. I guess that's the best time to
go, when you're comfortable and cared
for. I really hope you don't feel sad
for too long. Tell your mom and dad
that we will all be sending big waves
of love from over here.

★ **Cordelia** to Dru

THANK YOU! I've never known anyone who
died before but I suppose it happens all the time.

★ **Dru** to Cordelia

Yeah, I guess it does, but even
though dying is quite ordinary it
still feels so huge and shocking.

We were all quiet for weeks after my grandma passed away.

It doesn't seem right to mention the cabaret, but I'm so glad it went well.

★ **Cordelia** to Dru
And it doesn't seem right to mention Curly the puppy, but how is he?

★ **Dru** to Cordelia
He's poopy – all over the place, but he's fast asleep right now and looking *so* **ADORABLE**...! Aunt Zillah loves him and says she might get one, too. It would be good exercise for her. Oh no! I just heard Mom get up to use the bathroom. If she catches me on the computer at this time, I'll be banned for **WEEKS**. Better go xx

Thank goodness for Dru! I feel like I can get through the day now that I've written to her. I hope she doesn't get banned from emailing. What would I do without her words of wisdom?

When I come off the computer I call Fiona to tell her the news about GT but her phone is switched off so I ask Dad if I can go up to the allotment and see Joe.

'After lunch,' he says, 'Sandwich first. We should all try to eat something.'

That afternoon, Mum leaves for Gran's house. She has to do what she calls 'making arrangements'. I don't know what that involves but it doesn't sound like fun. She says she'll be back by the end of the week.

'Will you and Dad take care of each other for a few days?' she asks, after we've all managed to eat something and are saying goodbye.

'Of course we will,' I tell her.

Dad loads the car up with snacks and then holds Mum very tightly before she climbs in and drives away.

We are still waving when Dad says, 'I've got a plan that will really cheer Mum up when she gets back.'

'What is it?' I ask, feeling excited. I'd do almost anything to make Mum feel better right now.

'Before I tell you I've just got to call Uncle Ed and Uncle Dave because the plan depends on their help.'

'Can't you tell me first?' I ask, frowning.

But Dad is already pressing buttons on his mobile and he just raises his hand gently to signal that I'll have to wait. How FRUSTRATING. Then he disappears into the pub and shuts the door in a way that tells me I mustn't listen in, and he doesn't come out for AGES so I have to keep myself busy by tidying up the lunch things, or I'll burst with curiosity.

By the time Dad comes back into the kitchen I have turned on the radio and got out my sketchbook. I'm doing some doodling with my pencils to keep my mind occupied.

'Tell me!' I say, tugging on his jumper impatiently as he walks past me to get to the kettle.

Dad clicks the kettle on and then turns to me, rubbing his hands together.

'Well,' he begins, and I can tell that he's pleased with his plan, 'the new flat upstairs is nearly ready for you and Mum to move into and I thought it would be great to get it finished for when she returns.'

This is PERFECT.

'It'll be like a fresh start, won't it?' I say.

'For both of you,' Dad agrees.

'What about you?' I ask. 'You need cheering up, too.'

'It'll help me as well,' he explains. 'Once you two are living upstairs in the new flat, I can start getting this cottage fixed up. When that's done I can move in and get out of that flipping caravan.'

Dad tells me that as soon as he explained the situation to Uncle Ed and Uncle Dave they promised to be with us immediately so they can arrange some time out of their jobs and pack suitcases.

Uncle Ed and Uncle Dave are Dad's brothers. They're both big and jolly and they always fill the house with cheerfulness, so I can't wait for them to arrive. We could do with a bit of jolliness right now.

'Can I pop up to the allotment and see Joe now?' I ask.

Dad agrees. 'But keep your phone switched on and be back by four o'clock. It'll be getting dark then,' he says, 'and your uncles will be here.'

He gives me some chocolate brownies that he made yesterday to take with me, and a big flask of tea to share with Joe. I need to talk to someone NOW, and Fiona's phone is still switched off, so catching Joe at the allotment is my best idea.

I wander through the village, past the teashop

with the stuffed parrot in the window that makes me itch, past the closed-down shoe shop and the closed-down post office and Driscoll's Discount, which has a removal van outside. HOORAY!

But walking along quietly like this allows the empty, cold-jacket-potato-feeling to come back. Sad, grey thoughts about GT sneak back into my mind. I just don't understand how someone can be here one day and have totally DISAPPEARED the next. It makes me think that one day I'll be gone, too, and there is so MUCH that I want to do before then. When I start thinking this way it leads to worrying that Mum and Dad will be gone one day, as well, and then I feel like crying and I want to get to Joe's allotment quickly, to enjoy the chocolate brownies and the peace and quiet, and see his cheery-making smile. He will have something helpful and wise to say about it all, I'm sure. He usually does.

When I get there I ring the bell on its big iron spring and walk straight in, like I always do, but OH MY GOODNESS I wish I hadn't because right there in front of me, next to the blackberry bush are Joe and Fiona…

KISSING!

They jump apart and Joe mumbles something about picking the last of the blackberries but Fiona doesn't say anything, she just looks at me with her mouth in a big O and I think I must have the same expression on my face so we stand frozen for a millisecond, but it feels like HOURS, looking like a pair of Os until I shout in little tearful sobs that jump out of me, 'My…granny…just…DIED and you're KISSING?' and I RUN.

I don't even think, I just run and run. So that's why Fiona's phone was switched off. She was hiding from me. I hear them calling after me and shouting for me to 'hang on!' and 'wait!' but I don't stop. I just want to get far away from them. I'm all shaken up inside and there are HUGE FAT TEARS rolling down my cheeks and streaking my face. Tea is spilling out of the flask and leaving a wet trail behind me, and the chocolate brownies are getting swung around and mushed up in their bag. I grip them tightly and fly back down the hill towards home.

On the way I glimpse Mrs Driscoll bossing her removal men around but I don't even think *good riddance*. I hardly notice her. I hardly notice anything. I rush upstairs and hide in my old room.

What will happen now? If Joe and Fiona are going to be all LOVEY and KISSY they won't want me hanging around like the last sandwich left on the plate. I'm going to be ABANDONED by both of them just when I'm all mixed up about GT, and Mum isn't here and Dad is too busy to speak to me. How will I face my uncles when they arrive? If they see my pink puffy eyes and my swollen nose they'll know that I've been having a BIG BLUB.

I sit on the bare mattress and blow my nose. Then I lie down, switch off my phone, close my eyes and count my breathing. In, 1, out, 1…in, 2, out, 2. I'm trying to feel calmer but my thoughts are flying around like socks in a washing machine.

All GT's things have gone from the room and the bed is stripped and ready to move. Her grumpiness and her muddled mind are just a memory now, like the people and places in Mr Phillip's photographs.

Life has turned a million somersaults in less than a day. GT has gone, and now it looks like I might lose Joe AND Fiona as friends. I don't want our friendships suddenly to be GONE, like GT. I don't want them to be over, to be something that USED TO BE, like a sad memory.

Mrs Driscoll and her removal van have probably gone by now. Her nastiness is just a memory. The Halloween Cabaret is another memory now. Auntie Deirdre is a memory that's fading — I can just about remember her skirts that rustled and her red lipstick. And even now, seeing Joe and Fiona kissing has become a memory — a raw, fresh, painful memory. Everything becomes a memory very quickly, I suppose. You can't stop things from finishing and changing because time just doesn't work that way. But why do all MY memories seem to be sad, or else just plain TRAUMATICALLY AWFUL?

I must've fallen asleep because I wake up very muddled and notice that it's nearly dark outside. I smell pasta sauce cooking and hear the distant chatter of grown-ups. Of course! My uncles are here. I wash my face and hands before I go down. My face is still blotchy and puffed up but I can't hide up here forever.

19

'When did you get home?' Dad asks, looking
surprised when I slip quietly into the pub kitchen.

'Ages ago,' I say, flipping my hand and doing
my best to sound like nothing in particular has
happened.

I can't tell him what ACTUALLY happened or
I'll BLUB again.

My uncles must've popped out to get more stuff
from Uncle Ed's car because they come in from the
back yard just then, carrying toolbags.

'Hey, Cordelia!' they both shout, and open their
big hairy arms for a cuddle. I can't help smiling
because they're so jolly and full of love. Uncle Ed
has long hair and a big ginger beard. He runs a
campsite in the summer and plays the drums in a
folk band in the winter. He always looks like he's
just come in from a long walk in the countryside –
rosy-cheeked and twinkly-eyed. Uncle Dave is
taller than Uncle Ed and my dad. His hair is very

short, like Dad's. He's skinny like Dad, too, because he cycles a lot. He says it helps with the stress of working in an office. Neither of my uncles is married but Uncle Ed lives with his girlfriend, Freya, who teaches Archaeology at a university and digs pots out of the ground and then cleans them with tiny brushes, like on television.

'Are you going to help get the flat ready to cheer Mum up?' I ask them both.

'We certainly are,' says Uncle Dave. 'She'll be a happy lady when she sees it.'

Dad interrupts us by pulling an enormous lasagne out of the cooker and plonking it on the table in front of us.

'Knives and forks, please, Coco,' he calls, throwing his oven glove over his shoulder.

'Coming up!' I call back, and for a little while I forget all about my sad memories and just listen to my uncles and my dad telling each other all their news.

That night Dad sleeps on the floor in our tiny living room again and my uncles share the caravan. Before I fall asleep I look across at Mum's pillow. I hope she's all right. I don't like the thought of her being all alone in GT's cold house, probably feeling sad. I want her to come home.

♥

When I wake up in the morning I stare at the ceiling and think about Fiona and Joe kissing. Have I lost both of my friends now? Will they stick together like glue and shut me out? The grey, scooped-out-jacket-potato feeling is inside me again. The next thing I think about is GT. Is she happy and peaceful, wherever she is? And what about Mum? Has she woken up cold and lonely? Has she got something nice for breakfast? It isn't a cheerful start to the day but Dad has promised to cook porridge for everyone this morning. Perhaps that will help, especially with lots of honey.

Downstairs in the kitchen I tell Dad about the grey, empty-potato feeling I have while he stirs his lovely porridge.

'That's because you're grieving,' he tells me.

'What does that mean, exactly?' I ask.

Dad puts the honey pot on the table and passes me a spoon.

'When we are separated from someone,' he explains, 'like when they die, we have to slowly let go of them and accept that they aren't coming back. It can take a long time to feel normal again, so don't worry.'

My dad is very good at explaining complicated feelings. Sometimes he's even wiser than Dru or her Aunt Zillah, or Joe.

'Is it the same for people who are still alive?' I ask him, thinking about Fiona and Joe. 'I mean, if you had a friend but they weren't going to be your friend any more EVER because they'd found someone else they wanted to be with all the time. Would you grieve about that?'

'Yes, it's likely you would,' he says, 'except that when people are alive we can still talk to them.'

OF COURSE! I suddenly remember Dru's advice. I have to be brave and have dialogue with Joe and Fiona. But this time there are two of them and only one of me and I have NO idea what I want to say. I'll just HAVE to try otherwise all I will remember is the shock of seeing them kissing, and I can't let that be my final memory of my friendship with Joe and Fiona.

While Dad and my uncles get to work on

finishing off the kitchen and bathroom in the new flat I write to Dru again. I tell her about seeing Fiona and Joe kissing and crying until my face was like a marshmallow that got left out in the rain.

Dru is online. She must be having another of her sleepless nights. I finish by asking:

How can I make my memories feel happy instead of like **TERRIBLE TRAUMAS**?

★ **Dru** to Cordelia

```
That's a tough question. I'll ask
Aunt Zillah. She's soaking in the
bathtub - she stays up late sometimes,
like me, but she promises not to tell
Mom that I'm online. Back in a minute!
```

So I wait, and while I'm waiting I bite the nail on my right thumb – I try to bite just this one nail so that the others will grow but it doesn't always work, and I still bite the others. Dru comes back just in time to stop me starting on the other thumbnail.

★ **Dru** to Cordelia

```
I just whispered to Aunt Zillah
```

through the bathroom door. She is a geeeenius! She says you just have to **DECIDE** that a memory is happy, not sad. That way you'll see the positive side of most situations.

★ **Cordelia** to Dru

But I might be about to lose my friends because they've gone all **LOVEY** with each other.

★ **Dru** to Cordelia

I told her that but she says that might not happen at all, you've just decided it before you've even spoken to them. She said, 'You are in charge of your own mind, so you must be in charge of the feelings that you have.'

Oh Jeez! Here comes Mom. Bye!

Can I really DECIDE how I'm going to feel about something? This is a completely new idea to me and it will need time to soak into the squashy sponge of my brain.

After lunch I'm allowed to start arranging my new bedroom. It only needed vacuuming and the furniture moving in because we painted it a few weeks ago. It's so BIG and bright – I already know I'm going to LOVE it.

All my precious bits and pieces – my sewing patterns, books and DVDs, sixty-three copies of *Stars and Screen* magazine, jewellery and handbags from second-hand shops and car boot sales, shoes that are too small, T-shirts that are too small, pieces of fabric that I will make into something ONE DAY, books, notebooks, sketchbooks, more sketchbooks, pencils and paints and pens and my film star posters – are soon stacked around the bed waiting to go onto my new shelves. I love doing this job. Choosing where to put things and moving them to just the right place is so relaxing – it's like THERAPY.

By the time I'm ready to put my posters of Audrey Hepburn and Rita Hayworth on the wall I have had a good, LONG think and I'm beginning to understand what Dru's Aunt Zillah means.

I've already DECIDED that finding Joe and

Fiona kissing is a terrible memory and that they will abandon me but, if they're happy about being lovey with each other, and if I could DECIDE to be happy about it, too, it will change to being a good memory, one that's quite sweet and romantic. When I think like that, I can see that they might not abandon me at all, as long as I don't get into a stroppy-pants mood and panic about them seeing each other. Perhaps Aunt Zillah is right and I DO have control of my own mind. I don't suppose I can make EVERYTHING seem good. For example, finding out that Granny had died while we were at the Halloween Cabaret might never be a happy memory. I'm not saying that this will work ALL the time. I will probably still have moments of deep DRAMARAMA and sobbing, but it has to be worth trying, doesn't it?

Somehow, my thought waves must have reached Joe and Fiona, because at four o'clock I see them from the upstairs window, coming to knock on our door. It's getting dark but it is unmistakably them. Immediately, I forget EVERYTHING I have decided and go back to feeling scared. What if they've come to say they don't need me any more? Then I'll have no best friend and no second best friend either, apart from Dru, who is on the other side of the world, so that doesn't count. Oh dear! I count my breathing again: in, 1, out, 1. In, 2, out, 2. I try to steady my frightened FLAPPING.

Dad and my uncles are busy hammering the kitchen into place, so they can't hear Joe and Fiona knocking on the door. What if I ignored them and pretended I was out? That would give me more time to think. But it would also give me more time to fret and worry. OH DEAR! I'll just have to open the door. I'm still counting my breathing as I scurry downstairs. In, 1, out, 1. In, 2, out, 2. I turn the door handle and pull, slowly, wanting to be calm and mature but I am SO pleased when I see that they're smiling that I just blurt everything out.

'I'm SORRY about yesterday,' I say. 'I'm sorry about running away like a crazy person when I saw you. It's just…my…granny…' (my voice goes chokey and stuttery) 'died and I…phoned but you…weren't there so I…went…to…find…' (I am starting to cry in little dry sobs – SOBLETS, that I didn't expect) '…Joe and' (sob) '…there you' (sob) '...both were' (sob) '...KISSING!' (SOB SOB!)

Fiona looks confused and sorry and sympathetic all at the same time. Joe is frowning, like he's totally puzzled and surprised and sad for me. There are about a hundred expressions on their faces all mixed and muddled, like a big salad of emotions. Fiona gives me a wraparound hug and I let all my soblets gush out because I can't hold them in any longer.

'We called and called you but we didn't think you wanted to talk,' says Joe from behind her.

I pull my phone out of my pocket, sniffing, and see that it's still switched off from when I lay down on the bed yesterday. When I turn it back on I see that I've had about a ZILLION calls and messages from them and I just didn't think to check – I was so stuck inside my own little bubble.

'When I saw you at the allotment,' I explain, managing to control my sniffles, 'I thought you were both going to cut me out and not be my friends any more.'

Fiona sighs, saying, 'Why would we throw our best friend away just because we like each other? That's bonkers, Cordelia.'

She kisses me on both cheeks and squeezes me close.

'Completely bonkers,' Joe agrees, and he wraps his arms around both of us and we stand in a big tight hug while I have another little sob.

A few minutes later we are all sitting in the little kitchen. I get out some biscuits and pour us all some juice, then I tell them EVERYTHING that happened after the Halloween Cabaret and they both just listen and listen, although I have to repeat some of it because of the noise from upstairs, where my dad and uncles are still bashing the new kitchen into place.

Joe reaches over and squeezes my hand saying, 'I'm glad I got to dance with your gran.'

I think about him dancing round and round the kitchen with GT, and I smile and decide that it will always be one of my BEST memories.

20

Dad says that I can have the day off school on Monday, if I want to, but I'd rather go in and keep busy, even though I didn't sleep very well in my new bedroom because I was worried about Mum, and I still look a MESS from all that crying.

Things are patched up nicely with Joe and Fiona but I still have that grey, cold-potato feeling because I still haven't quite let go and allowed GT to move on wherever she is going next. Dad keeps telling me that this is perfectly normal and that the feeling will shrink away with time.

Because it's Monday we all have to go straight to the main hall for assembly. After saying, 'Good morning, school,' and making a few of the usual announcements about keeping off the playing field when it's muddy and not smoking ANYWHERE, Mr Okenden reports that the Halloween Cabaret made A THOUSAND POUNDS towards books for the Head Space. We give a big cheer. I manage to cheer and smile, too, even though I have a big pink fish-face from a whole weekend of sobbing and I'm so TIRED from all the emotional drama.

Then Mr Okenden's expression drops like jelly poured into a bucket – the corners of his mouth flump down and his eyebrows follow them. He holds up a copy of the local newspaper, the *Wellminster Weekly*. It looks like the reporter who went to Mrs Driscoll's meeting has written about us. Hooray!

'However,' he continues, in his boomy voice, 'there was some unacceptable behaviour at a meeting held before the dress rehearsal. All those who attended that meeting — you know who you are — will remain in their seats. The rest of the school may go.'

And OF COURSE, we know that he means our BRILLIANTLY SUCCESSFUL PROTEST. So everyone involved in the Halloween Cabaret has to stay behind and get an ear-bending about disrupting the meeting and dragging the name of the school through the mud, and how our behaviour has been reported in the local paper.

Fiona whispers to me, 'He thinks we'll get a bad report from the school inspectors. That's all he cares about.'

She's probably right. And how DARE he take all the money that OUR cabaret made and then tell us off? Mr Okenden is TREACHEROUS and SLIPPERY. He is a SNAKE.

'Cordelia Codd, Fiona Kidney, Peter Skanski and Joe Grover, stand please,' he says.

We stand up. Fiona is next to me. Peter is further down our row of seats. Joe is a little way back.

'I have a letter in my hand from a parent who has named you as the ringleaders of the protest. You were on school premises without permission and you interrupted a meeting that had been arranged by the Parent Teacher Association. You set a bad example to the *entire* school, to the staff, the other pupils and members of the public who attended.'

My furious red feeling is starting to boil. I can't believe what he is saying. And who would write a letter like that, anyway?

I look around the hall and, *QUELLE SURPRISE!* I see Becky and Ruby peering through the glass door, sticking their tongues out at us and pointing.

I nudge Fiona and whisper, 'I bet THEY wrote it.'

She glances towards the door and gasps. Her

eyes go wide and boggly as she realises that I am probably bing-bang on the truth button.

'It's their revenge for being kicked off the cabaret,' she whispers back. 'Pretend you don't care.'

She sticks her chin in the air and puts on her heroic face. Lifting your chin up at moments of crisis can really help you feel brave.

'Stop talking!' Mr Okenden yells, and our knees start knocking, but our chins are still high.

'You four will be in detention tomorrow night. I expect to see you in this hall as soon as the final bell goes. Now, go back to class!'

Everyone agrees that this detention is OUTRAGEOUS.

'There wouldn't have been a Halloween Cabaret AT ALL if we hadn't protested,' I say.

'And he wouldn't have that one thousand pounds!' Joe adds.

Word soon gets around school that Becky and Ruby wrote the letter so NO ONE speaks to them.

At breaktime, Fiona and I sit in our usual sunny spot by the car park and share some juicy plums she's brought for a snack. She asks if I'm feeling OK about Granny and I tell her about the grey potato feeling that Dad says will go away eventually but then admit that, 'At the moment I feel mostly RED and FUMING about these detentions.'

Fiona agrees. 'We mustn't let Ruby and Becky think that we're bothered by them. That's exactly what they want.'

She offers me another plum and I can't refuse. They are DELISH.

'Can I just double-check one other thing with you, though?' she asks

'Of course. What?' I mumble through a mouthful of plum.

'Well, you don't *really* mind if Joe and I go out together, do you?'

I shake my head. I nearly start crying again, this time with relief because my decision to be happy about Fiona and Joe is working, after a slightly wobbly start yesterday. I don't feel upset about it ONE LITTLE BIT. I swallow the rest of my plum before speaking. 'The timing was a bit weird,' I admit, 'because of Granny dying, but I'm glad it's Joe you've chosen as a boyfriend. At least he's nice, and he'll be far too busy looking after his cabbages and potatoes to see much of you, so we'll have plenty of time to do best-friend stuff.'

Fiona giggles. 'Of course we will! You're

my best friend in the whole world, Cordelia. I wouldn't abandon you just because I've got a boyfriend.' She squeezes my hand. 'And you're absolutely right about Joe. It will be vegetables first, girlfriend second.' She shrugs her shoulders. 'But that's fine. I've got other things to do, too, right?'

I nod.

Fiona remembers something. 'Will you be coming to the fireworks display on Friday night?' she asks.

I hesitate. 'With you and Joe? I'm not sure I want to be a gooseberry, if it's a date.'

'No,' she says quickly, 'with me and Joe and Jamila and Alice and about half the class. We'll all be there together.'

That changes my mind immediately.

'DEFINITELY!' I say. 'And shall I ask if you can stay for a sleepover at mine afterwards? I want you to see my new room.'

'Yes, please!' she says, sounding VERY excited. 'As long your mum and dad don't mind having visitors when you've just lost your gran?'

I tell her that I think it'll be fine but I'll check with Mum and Dad first.

We head back in to be taught French very BADLY by Mrs Crowther-Dupont, and to watch her doing hideous knitting.

♥

As soon as they hear what's happened, Lennox, Gregor, Alice and Jamila all come and find me to say, 'I'm sorry about your gran.'

Peter hands me some chocolate at afternoon registration. He says he's sorry to hear about Granny, too, and adds, 'I think there might be a bit of a surprise for Mr Okenden at tomorrow's detention.'

'What's that?' I ask.

He puts his finger to his lips. 'Top secret. Wait and see,' he says. 'It'll cheer you up, I promise.'

I might BURST with curiosity before tomorrow.

That evening I write and tell Dru that the upset with Fiona and Joe was temporary, and that we've had a dialogue and it's all fine. I tell her about my uncles' noisy work on the flat, getting things ready for when Mum comes back, and, OF COURSE, I tell her how we are in a completely unfair detention over the protest. I remember to finish with:

Did you and Esther manage to avoid **PUMPKIN POISONING**?

Love you!!

C

Xx

She doesn't write back that night. Either she is managing to sleep better or she was nabbed by her mum for using the computer at crazy o'clock and has been BANISHED. I hope not because I'll HAVE to report to her about tomorrow's detention.

Apart from the little computer desk, the cottage is bare now. All the furniture has gone up to the new flat or been given away to a charity shop. It's cold in here and smells a bit damp, and the grey, cold-potato feeling creeps inside me again when I look over to the corner where GT sat with her typewriter, tapping away. I shiver, take a deep breath and DECIDE that this will be a good memory of my slightly dotty granny.

I look around once more. I don't want to forget how it looked before Dad and the decorators renovate it and make it new again. It's a little part of my history, I suppose.

Uncle Ed and Uncle Dave have gone into
Wellminster this evening, so it's just me and Dad
and an ENORMOUS curry for dinner.

'I hope Mum's OK in GT's dark little house,' I
tell him. 'Will she be having nice things to eat?'

'She's fine,' he promises. 'I spoke to her this
afternoon. And we'll feed her lots of good things
when she gets back.'

I hear him talking to Mum on the phone again
later, just before bedtime. He's being gentle and
calm and he doesn't give away any clues about the
new flat. He pretends that everything is normal
and boring here but actually, two extra builders
are arriving tomorrow to help Dad and Uncle Ed
and Uncle Dave. They're staying until everything
is done because it's the last day before Mum
comes home. Dad is paying them with lunch and
dinner and a bottle of wine. He's doing all this
AND helping with the decorating too, AND
taking care of me, but Mum has no idea that all
this is going on. I hope she'll understand that
he's doing all this work because he LOVES her.
I don't push in on his phone call and ask to talk

to her because they sound quite serious. Instead I write:

GIVE MUM A BIG KISS
FROM ME

on a piece of paper and hold it up so Dad can't miss it. He smiles and gives me a thumbs-up, then I leave the paper next to him so that he doesn't forget.

When he comes off the phone I tell him about the detention, but he isn't cross. He says that he's on my side over the whole protest thing. My dad is really cool sometimes.

Tonight I can use the new bathroom in the flat for the first time. It's quite luxurious compared to the old one. I have a WONDERFUL bubbly soak, and then sleep like a warm kitten.

21

When the final bell sounds at school on Tuesday, Fiona, Peter and I meet Joe in the main corridor and make our way to the hall, where Mr Okenden is waiting for us. He reads our names out, then says, 'Right. You can each stand in a corner of the hall and face outwards. You will stand in silence.'

HONESTLY! What a waste of time.

We are standing in our corners and I'm wondering if I'll collapse in a bored heap of DESPAIR before an hour has passed when the doors swing open and in walks...well... EVERYONE. Every single person who was involved in the Halloween protest has come. Mr Okenden looks up from his table.

'What's this, another protest?' he says. 'Everyone out!'

But nobody moves. They stand in the middle of the hall and face outwards. They stand in silence, right behind us and my heart is flying around with a sort of excited happiness. This is what Peter meant. This was his top secret surprise. AMAZING.

I peek over my shoulder from the corner that I've been stuffed into and see Lennox take a letter out of his blazer pocket. He reads it to Mr Okenden.

'Everyone here supports the protest that took place last week,' he begins. 'We were all defending our right, and everyone else's right, to celebrate Halloween, and also our right to protest peacefully. We will not be divided from our friends. We are proud of them and we will stand beside them.'

Mr Okenden has gone a very dark shade of purple.

'Very well,' he bellows, full of windy bluster. 'You can all stand in silence, and we'll see how many of you are still here to support your *friends* at the end of the hour.'

But of course, nobody leaves for the WHOLE detention. We stay still and silent apart from a few accidental burps and farts that make us all giggle. Not one single person chickens out, and at the end, when Mr Okenden dismisses us and scurries back to his office – probably so that he doesn't have to admit that he was wrong about us sticking together – Peter announces that Bessie, from

Bessie's Bakery, has heard about our mass detention and is providing free crisps, cakes and milkshakes RIGHT NOW, for anyone who can get there.

Everyone starts texting and calling their parents to get permission to go to Bessie's, and within half an hour most of us are squeezed into the room at the back of her cafe, eating crisps and cake and drinking her special fruity milkshakes.

'There's too much bad stuff said about you young people these days,' she announces. 'It isn't fair. Not many people would have stood up for their rights like you did, and stuck with their friends. I think that deserves a little party.'

'Three cheers for Bessie!' shouts Jason in his big, strong opera-singer voice, and we all join in with a cheer that rattles the windows.

HIP HIP HOORAY! HIP HIP HOORAY!
HIP HIP HOORAY!

Bessie giggles and blushes, saying, 'Just tidy up after yourselves when you go.'

Joe stands on a chair and bangs on the biscuit tin with the wooden spoon, **CHANG CHANG CHANG**, to get everyone's attention. 'Look this way, everyone,' he calls. We turn and look. He puts down the biscuit tin and counts, '1,2,3…' Then takes a photo with his phone.

'I'm just sending that picture to Ruby and Becky,' he says. 'Tell me if you think this message is OK.' He reads:

> Hi both. We're just being treated
> to free food and drinks @ Bessie's.
> Thanks for the detention! From all
> of us.

We give another big cheer, then Joe presses SEND.

'That'll give them both something to think about,' Fiona says, and I have to agree. I know that Becky CAN be nice if she tries because I saw her being sweet to the old folks in Goldenboughs, and I know that Ruby is only horrid because she's a bit messed-up, but they still need to learn that there are consequences when you treat people badly, so I don't feel THAT sorry for them really.

We forget about Ruby and Becky and carry on chatting and giggling, munching crisps and slurping milkshakes. Joe and Fiona don't sit close together, like some girlfriends and boyfriends would. They talk to lots of people and don't behave like they're glued to each other. This is a good sign, I think.

When people eventually start to go home I'm sitting with Peter near the window. We are debating whether *Son of Frankenstein* is a better film than *Return of Frankenstein*.

'But *Son of Frankenstein* has the best line,' I argue.

'I suppose you're right,' he agrees, and pulls a poppy-eyed, scary face saying, 'It's alive! It's alive!'

I squeak with excitement. 'That's the line! That creepy moment when Baron von Frankenstein's monster starts to move and electricity is whizzing around his laboratory. It's brilliant!'

Peter nods and smiles, and suddenly I remember something.

'You haven't told me!' I say.

'Told you what?'

'About your BIG DREAM. Do you know what it is yet?'

Peter looks down into his milkshake and stirs it with his stripy drinking straw.

'Actually, yes, I've been thinking about it.'

'So?' I prompt him, jiggling impatiently in my seat.

He takes a deep breath. 'I want to be an architect,' he tells me. 'I want to build really amazing houses that use solar power and all that eco-friendly stuff.'

And I can see from the way that he looks straight into my eyes when he's talking that he means it.

'You'll be BRILLIANT,' I tell him.

'Thanks…yes…I think I could be pretty good at it if I work hard.'

And this time he doesn't sound pompous at all, he just sounds…well…certain. I like boys to be certain about what they want to do. It's very attractive.

Oh dear!

I have just realised something else, something HUGE. My eyes are stuck, looking into Peter's for a millisecond longer than normal. I feel my face turn SCARLET and look down quickly at the table, which is sticky and covered in crisp crumbs.

OH MY GIDDY GOODNESS! It would all FIT. When I'm living in Paris or Berlin or Milan, or wherever, sitting in a very different sort of café, watching a busy, beautiful street instead of looking out over the bins behind the bus station, and different languages are being spoken all around me, Peter would fit PERFECTLY into the picture. He is interesting and sometimes funny, and very, very clever. He is getting quite stylish and, BEST OF ALL, he is usually busy, so I wouldn't have to be with him EVERY day. He is EXACTLY the kind of boyfriend I need.

'It's dark, I'd better get home,' I tell him, and leave as quickly as I can. I need some air and some thinking space to process this MASSIVE moment.

I lie awake for AGES. Not because I'm full of sugar from Bessie's treats but because now that I've decided that Peter will be the right boyfriend for me I haven't a clue WHAT to do about it! My brain is WHIZZING with ideas but they all seem RUBBISH. Should I:

a) Just tell him that I think he'll make a good boyfriend? No. Too unromantic

b) Ask Fiona to tell him that I'm interested? No. Even though she's my best friend, she would get too excited and make me rush things.

c) Send him a letter tied with a ribbon that smells of perfume? No. **Ridiculous** and old-fashioned.

d) Text him? **Unthinkable,** you just don't do this sort of thing with a text.

e) Email? Ditto – just as bad as texting. A big **No**!

f) Just be his friend and hope he tries to kiss me again? Maybe.

g) *Kiss him, so he knows I like him? Too risky. What if he's gone off me? He might run away or shout, 'Yuck!' or something. That would be Excruciatingly bad for my confidence.*

I sneak to the computer. Dru will know what to do. First I read her reply.

★ **Dru** to Cordelia

Fantastic news about Fiona and Joe. I knew you could do it! You turned things around so that they look shiny and happy instead of miserable. That's **HUGE**. And...wow! Your detention friends are heroes! It's like the story of Spartacus. D'you know that one?

Good news from here - Esther and I managed to avoid eating Halloween pumpkin. Phew!

Nearly bad news - Mom caught me online late at night but Aunt Zillah

covered for me. She said she'd asked
me to find something on the internet
for her about growing winter cabbages.
Hooray for Aunt Zillah and her
imaginary cabbages!

   Love you!

   D xx

I am just about to ask her how I should talk to
Peter but I stop myself, my fingers hover over the
keyboard. It feels too new and uncertain. What
if I've made a silly mistake and he isn't the right
sort of boyfriend for me AT ALL? I don't want
to tell ANYONE, not even Dru. I would feel so
EMBARRASSED if I woke up tomorrow and the
feeling I have about him had disappeared.

But, of course, the next day, the feeling hasn't gone
away at all. I am just as muddled, and now also very
tired from lack of sleep. However, I have woken
up in our beautiful, completely finished flat. I can't
WAIT to see Mum's reaction when she gets home.

   'Is Mum coming back today?' I ask Dad when we

both shuffle into the kitchen for breakfast.

'Yes, this evening,' he tells me, and he starts to organise some toast and jam. 'Your uncles are leaving this morning, though, so she'll have no idea what's been going on. She'll think the decorating fairies have been.'

We giggle at this idea because Uncle Dave and Uncle Ed walk in just then. They couldn't look LESS fairy-like. They are both wearing dark bathrobes with toothpaste smudges down the front and they both need a shave. Dave still has paint in his short hair and Ed's long hair looks like an explosion in a knitting wool factory – it's ALL OVER THE PLACE.

Everything in the flat, except my uncles, is clean and sparkling and cosy, and there is a sunny view across the road to the trees and the river beyond. Mum is going to love it!

I chatter with them for too long and have to rush for the bus. I just have time to ask Dad if I can go to the fireworks and then have Fiona to sleep over afterwards. He's fine with this, so I say goodbye to my uncles, give them a big thank-you hug and dash out of the door.

I spend most of the day trying very hard NOT to look at Peter or think about him. I am trying so hard to do this that I actually CONCENTRATE in Science instead of relying on Fiona to do the thinking for me. The result of this is that I quite enjoy the lesson, instead of just surviving until breaktime. The same thing happens in Maths and Geography. AMAZING. This makes the day pass quickly, and, before I know it, school is over and Fiona and Joe and I are heading back to Heckaby on the bus to see the fireworks.

When Fiona and I burst in full of FIREWORK EXCITEMENT, Mum and Dad are sitting in the living room of the new flat with mugs of tea and some flapjacks Dad has made. He has even managed to find time to put red roses in a vase on the coffee table. Mum is SO surprised and delighted with the way our new place looks that she is nearly crying.

I'm pleased to have her back safely and to know that she'll be eating Dad's lovely food again. Fiona and I are so happy tucking into the flapjacks and telling Mum all about school that we almost forget about the fireworks. Suddenly, we hear WHIZZ,

CRACKLE, PHIZZZLE from the playing field across the road.

'They've started!' Dad calls from the kitchen, and we have to rush to change out of our school clothes, get our jeans and jumpers on, and RUN.

Joe is already near the bonfire when we get there. Alice, Jasmin, Lennox and Gregor – and loads of other kids from the Halloween Cabaret – have arrived too. AND I spot Miss Wallcott, standing with Mr Finnegan. Fiona and I agree that they look PERFECT together but we promise each other that we won't tell anyone, because we don't want them to get teased at school by lentil-brains like Ruby and Becky.

When Peter arrives he comes and stands beside us and I feel a bit embarrassed – I just can't look at him without going pink, which is STUPID and ANNOYING. It probably seems like I'm being unfriendly. *Just RELAX, Cordelia,* I tell myself, but it isn't easy.

The grand finale of the fireworks display is SO loud that I have to put my fingers in my ears. It's a GIGANTIC round of explosions and bright lights and smoke. Squeals and oohs and aaahhhs and WOWs go up all around us. For a tiny village at the boring end of the universe, Heckaby certainly does GREAT fireworks.

Right at the finish, the sky becomes one big white DAZZLE and BANG for a second before it all stops and we are left coughing and laughing through the smoke. The smell of fireworks and wood smoke and the feel of the cold, muddy field under my wellies is perfect for a bonfire party. There are wafts of hot toffee apple, too, and chicken soup from a little stall nearby.

As the smoke clears I look around. Peter has gone. I don't know when he left. I've decided, although I'm still not sure what I'm going to say to him, that I HAVE to be brave and talk about my feelings. It's the scariest option from my list because he might reject me, but I'll just have to deal with that if it happens. I can't walk around school full of this stupid, embarrassed feeling all the time.

I leave the group and wander off, hoping I'll find him on his own – I don't want anyone to hear me make a complete fool of myself in front of a boy. Eventually I find him lying on his back along a big tree trunk near the children's playground. As I walk over I count my breathing. In, 1, out, 1…in, 2, out, 2.

He has his hood up and is gazing at the sky. I peer down at his face and wave.

'*Now is the time, Cordelia,* I tell myself. *You HAVE to say something.*' I'm ready, breathing deeply and slowly and about to open my mouth to speak when Peter sits up.

'There's something I need to tell you, Cordelia,' he says.

'Me too.' I add quickly, 'But you go first.'

'OK,' he begins, rubbing his hands together and then resting them on his knees and staring at the ground.

'Are you going to tell me that you're scared of fireworks?' I ask. 'It's OK. I won't tell anyone.'

Peter laughs and shakes his head.

'No, I love fireworks,' he says.

He's looking at me now, which is making me MORE nervous because he's quite close and he might kiss me, which I sort of want but I'm not CERTAIN about it and I think I'm going pink again so I'm glad it's dark. Then he just says it... straight out...and it's not what I was expecting AT ALL.

'I'm going back to my old school.'

My mouth has dropped open a bit. I close it,

swallow and choke out a reply. 'Oh…oh…I see…
oh…Really? Why?'

All my big ideas about sitting in a café in Paris
of Berlin or Milan or wherever, and him being
interesting and funny and clever and WITH
ME have just melted like cheese on a pizza and
stretched into a big confusing mess in my head. MY
HEAD IS FULL OF PIZZA CHEESE.

'They've given me a scholarship so Mum can
send me back without worrying about the money,'
he explains.

'Oh. That's great news, I suppose, isn't it?' I
mumble. 'Congratulations. I'll…I'll miss you.'

He reaches over and squeezes my hand.

'I'll miss you, too, Cordelia. Thank you for
helping me to sort out my wardrobe, and for putting
up with me being Peter Pompous Pants.'

I give a tiny gasp. 'Who told you that we used to
call you that?'

'Never mind,' he says. 'It was true. I hope I'm not
like that any more.'

'Oh…no…you're…quite OK…now,' I say,
realising that this doesn't sound like a compliment. 'I
mean, you're fine, you're…y'know…not pompous.'

Then he leans over and puts his lips on mine.

He keeps them there for a few seconds, just long enough for me to feel how warm they are, and I wish straight away that he hadn't because this was the PERFECT first kiss, exactly what I was hoping for, and now I'll think about that kiss A LOT when he won't be here to give me any more of them. What good is THAT?

We stand up quickly because we see my mum and dad leaving the bonfire and looking around for me.

'You wanted to tell me something, too,' he reminds me.

But I'm not going to say it. I'm not going to tell him that I'd like to sit in a café with him one day in Paris or Berlin or Milan or wherever. I'm not going to tell him because I can see that all that was just MY plan, me, in MY head, and it isn't the way things are going to work out – not for a while, anyway. I suppose I will have a boyfriend one day, and we will sit in cafes together in lovely places, but it's probably not THIS boy, and it's not yet.

'Oh, it was nothing,' I say, flipping my hand and breathing in deeply at the same time. 'I'd better go,' I say. 'When are you leaving?'

'This weekend,' he says. 'It's all a bit sudden. I've

got a lot of catching up to do with the coursework so they want me back as soon as possible.'

'I'd better say bye, then,' I say, giving a little wave.

He opens his arms and we fall into a hug.

'Don't forget your big dream,' I whisper in his ear. 'Don't forget that you're going to be the best architect in the world.'

'I won't forget. I promise,' he whispers back, squeezing me gently. 'I won't forget my dream and I won't forget you, Cordelia Codd.'

We step apart.

'Bye, Peter,' I say, feeling a funny lump in between my tonsils.

He smiles, 'Bye, Cordelia.'

I turn then and run back across the field until the lumpy throat feeling has gone and I can see where Mum and Dad are standing. I stop then, and look round, ready to give him one last wave, but he's already gone. I don't feel too upset, though, because I've already decided that this evening is going to be a good memory, not a big, sad disappointment or trauma, but a lovely moment when I decided NOT to fall madly in love and NOT to worry about having a boyfriend for a while longer. It's the night when I remember that what I really want is to be **the [*]⋆ GREATEST ✦✦ costume designer in the history of cinema** and that's the most important thing – that, and my lovely friends. Dru will be proud of me when I tell her – and it feels like I have SO much great news to give her this time. Or perhaps I'm just seeing things differently.

I call to Mum and Dad through the dark, 'I'm here!'

Mum spots me straight away and she and Dad both look relieved.

Did I just see them holding hands? I HOPE so.

'It's a bit cold for Dad to sleep in the caravan tonight,' I say. 'Can he sleep on our sofa?'

Mum smiles and shakes her head saying, 'Don't worry about Dad and me, Cordelia.'

She knows that I'm just trying to get them back together. She links her arm through Dad's, saying, 'We're making progress, aren't we?'

Dad nods and gives her a twinkly look.

He puts his free arm around my shoulder and whispers, 'Don't worry, the cottage will soon be renovated. I'll move in there before Christmas with a bit of luck.'

And I suppose that will have to do for now. I can't rush them.

'Wait a minute!' I suddenly shout. 'We forgot Fiona. We're having a sleepover, remember!'

We spin around and see Fiona running towards us.

'I've got news,' she calls.

'So have I,' I tell her, but my news about Peter will have to wait because Fiona is going to EXPLODE with excitement if I don't let her speak first.

'I was just talking to Mr Gampy,' she tells me.

I hadn't even spotted that he was here.

'He told me that he's writing a pantomime for Christmas and he needs singers and dancers and **loads** of costumes.'

I give a little squeak of excitement, but Fiona pauses, then says, 'You won't mind if I sing, will you? I mean, Mr Gampy might give Ruby and Becky another chance so I might have to sing with them. Would you be upset?'

I give a big, long sigh and shake my head.

'I'll be absolutely fine about it! I promise...And I'll NEVER be a clingy-girl again.'

She squeezes both my hands.

'Anyway,' I tell her, 'you'll be singing a solo this time, I'll bet.'

But she doesn't get time to reply because we both notice Jason with his mum and wave to them.

'Let me guess,' I whisper to Fiona, 'is Jason going to be the pantomime dame?'

'I think that's pretty certain, don't you?' she replies, rolling her eyes and laughing.

I give another excited little squeak, saying, 'Pantomime dames always have LOADS of costumes. They change about a ZILLION times.'

I think Fiona can read my mind.

'Why don't you have a chat with him and his mum?' she suggests. 'She'll never be able to make all those costumes by herself.'

And I have already stopped worrying about my mum and dad being not quite together (NQT), and about Peter leaving, and I HOPE that Granny can feel how excited I am about the future. Wherever she is I will always remember her with love. But right now I'm running as fast as I can across the field shouting, 'Jason! I need to talk to you about a dress…!'

Acknowledgements

Thank you to my lovely agent, Alice Williams, for being so calm and sensible, and to all the team at Orchard for getting Cordelia out into the world once more.

A Q&A with **CLAIRE O'BRIEN**
author of

CORDELIA CODD

It's Alive!

Did you ever fall out with your best friend at school?

Yes, once. She moved to a different school before we made up, which made me very sad for a while. I hope she found some new friends, like I did.

Do you like scary films?

Not SERIOUSLY scary ones, they give me bad dreams. I prefer to watch funny films or historical films with fabulous costumes.

Which funny films would you recommend for Halloween?

Try some of these:

The Witches (2005)

Hocus Pocus (1993)

Addams Family Values (1993)

Edward Scissorhands (1990)

Young Frankenstein (1974)

Carry on Screaming (1966)

Abbot and Costello meet the Mummy (1955)

Laurel and Hardy, Live Ghost & Habeas Corpus (1933)

How do you celebrate Halloween?

I get lots of treats ready for when the trick or treaters come knocking, and sometimes I carve a pumpkin head to light up and put in the window. I love spooky pumpkin heads!

If you went to a Halloween party what costume would you wear?

Something ghostly and pale. What would you like to wear?

Hi, Cordelia here!

Friendship is REALLY important but we all argue sometimes. Try these tips for having dialogue.

- Remember that you probably both want to be friends again, so that's a great start.

- Be brave and offer to talk about things.

- Be ready to listen. If you don't listen, you'll never understand what went wrong.

- Try to have EMPATHY – see things from your friend's point of view.

- Be ready to say sorry if you need to.

- Don't shout or even raise your voice. This is the time to keep your emotions calm.

- Try not to walk away. Listen, and then try to keep talking it through.

- If it helps, ask a friend you both trust to make sure that each of you gets a chance to say how you feel. Teachers can help, too.

If you find that you can't fix the friendship, don't be too sad. You were brave and tried to have dialogue, so move on feeling proud of yourself – new friends are never far away.